THE MANUSCRIPT

Eva Zeller was born in 1923 and lived until 1956 in the former East Germany. She has been awarded numerous prizes for her previous books, which include novels, short stories and poetry. She now lives in Berlin.

Eva Zeller

THE MANUSCRIPT

TRANSLATED FROM THE GERMAN BY
Nadia Lawrence

VINTAGE

Published by Vintage 2001

2 4 6 8 10 9 7 5 3 1

Copyright © Deutsche Verlags-Anstalt GmbH 1998
Translation copyright © Jonathan Cape 2000

Eva Zeller has asserted her right under the Copyright,
Designs and Patents Act 1988 to be identified as the
author of this work

First published in Great Britain by
Jonathan Cape 2000

Vintage
Random House, 20 Vauxhall Bridge Road,
London SW1V 2SA

Random House Australia (Pty) Limited
20 Alfred Street, Milsons Point, Sydney
New South Wales 2061, Australia

Random House New Zealand Limited
18 Poland Road, Glenfield, Auckland 10,
New Zealand

Random House (Pty) Limited
Endulini, 5A Jubilee Road, Parktown 2193,
South Africa

The Random House Group Limited Reg. No. 954009
www.randomhouse.co.uk

A CIP catalogue record for this book
is available from the British Library

ISBN 0 09 928408 1

Papers used by Random House are natural, recyclable
products made from wood grown in sustainable forests.
The manufacturing processes conform to the environ-
mental regulations of the country of origin

Printed and bound in Denmark by
Nørhaven A/S, Viborg

For my daughter, Susanne

The wide river lay white and frozen like a continent's tongue lapsed into silence.

Joseph Brodsky, *Less Than One*

It is actually quite impossible that this keen, this suffering consciousness should just suddenly come to an end and disappear from the world.

Imre Kertész, *Kaddish*

In the Italian rooms of the Hermitage, Bea's eye falls on a life-size, or should one say life-small, marble sculpture: Michelangelo's *Crouching Boy*. She stands in front of it for a long time, thinking that this is how Jacob must have crouched in his hiding place during the time that he was supposed not to exist: seven, eight years old, a boy who had to be invisible. Bea wishes she could at last find the courage to ask him about those leaden childhood years which he has never mentioned.

But when Jacob returns from the archaeology rooms, where he has been examining the prehistoric finds from the Siberian frost-graves, he is so full of enthusiasm that Bea yet again has to become his audience, patiently listening while he tells her all about the various burial objects that were dug up there, the weapons, the silvered mirrors, the great quantities of jewellery, the precious jars for food and drink during the journey. The most vivid description of all is of a perfectly preserved knotted rug, bordered all around with hunting scenes; in between the huntsmen and the deer one can quite clearly see waterlilies: 'Nymphaea,' Jacob says. He is usually reticent but he talks and talks, drawing with his finger on the tabletop, leaves as big as plates and long-stemmed flowers. He does not see the tears in Bea's eyes, the long-distance lenses through which she is looking at another Siberian frost-grave, one where people were buried not six thousand years but half a century ago; a grave which Bea, too, should long ago have talked about.

But how? Where should she begin? Better to say nothing, so she listens instead to a lecture about the traces of primeval plants. The voice is Jacob's; the hand is his hand, it touches her wristwatch. 'You haven't changed your watch to Russian time yet, have you?'

Bea shakes her head. He slips the watch from her wrist and moves the hands on two hours.

The main part in this love story is played by a woman who shall be called Bea, the diminutive form of Beate, and Beate means 'blessed'.

The house where Bea was born, where her mother, her grandfather and his father were born, the house in Grunewald, which the bombs of the Second World War spared, which was never looted nor ever in danger of falling into decay – this house now belongs to her. She's the sole heir. She is, officially, the recipient of a gift, as her grandfather bequeathed the house to her during his lifetime, avoiding inheritance tax. How much gift tax he paid was never discussed. Bea, the blessed.

Bea lives alone. No kith. No kin. Make sure you get married again, her grandmother said shortly before she died. Being on your own is no great shakes.

For many years Bea has left everything in the house unchanged. She wants it to stay the way it has always been. She does not have the time to turn things upside-down. Her work at school is exhausting, she will not be able to cope with it much longer.

3

One lovely autumn day, though, at half-term, goodness knows why, she feels she wants to make her grandparents' house really hers. All day long, she wanders through the rooms to sort out what should be kept and what given away. Should she sell the Swedish chest with the iron fittings, and the decrepit Chippendale pieces; should she give someone her grandparents' bedroom suite? But who would want it nowadays, the enormous black-varnished oak double bed, wardrobes on claw feet, the grim chests of drawers? And what is she going to do with the hunting scenes hung in heavy gilt frames, with the antlers on the walls and the clouded mirrors? She knows that she is going to find it very difficult to part from all the junk; each object which she scarcely noticed any more has all at once turned into a memory – a treasure even, if she were going to be sentimental about it.

No, she really must make some space here, otherwise she will suffocate. So she makes an appointment with the refuse collectors – they want to come right away – and she begins, for she has to begin somewhere, by clearing out the attic, which is full of angles and corners and like a theatre prop room. There are oil lamps, with shades and without; the casing of a magic lantern, into which, Grandmother used to say, you could put colourful pictures, upside-down, and it would conjure them onto the tiles of a stove; the clock pendulum, now with a beautiful patina, which used to strike the hours of childhood and reverberated long afterwards. Picture frames lean

4

one against another, and on the top is a gutted wireless out of which the Führer's voice used to shriek: Grandfather would cover his ears and say it was a donkey's bray, aiming high and ending miserably. She trips over a box with sand in it, a fire-beater leaning against the side, and a wooden leg which was strapped on by one of her ancestors after the 1870–71 war, as the story went in the family. Little heaps of wood shavings show woodworms have been busy.

A telescope stands on a tripod; wherever one focused it one would see the soft wrappings of dust and time. The attic is the place for remnants, for the sediment of history. In a suitcase with wooden bands are tin soldiers armed with every kind of weapon, wearing helmets, charging, taking aim, firing, kneeling, men and officers crashing to the ground, little guns and field kitchens; and the buckled tracks of a model railway, metal engines, carriages, goods and coal trucks, most of them with the wheels missing. Here is Bea's wooden horse; she can't find the wooden board with the wheels which used to be attached to it. Shouting 'Gee up!' and 'Ha!' she used to drag it around behind her; it fell over the threshold of every doorway, crashed into every chair leg, and at every corner stood a little goblin and he starts talking to her now and tells her it's no use throwing this horse onto the rubbish tip: childhood is like that, it catches up with you, with or without wheels.

Bea wants to go into the little room where they used to smoke the hams and sausages; a sledge cover is hanging there, with rusty eyelets, and behind it are

5

stacks of boxes full of books, magazines, newspapers. On one of the boxes is her name. With the affectionate ending, Beatchen. Underneath dog-eared picture books and fairy tales, under colouring books and school books and bits and pieces of rubbish, between dominoes and ludo counters, lies a large sealed A5 envelope, on which is also her name: Beate. Under that, in large block capitals: FRAU HILLER'S NOTES.

Who is Frau Hiller?

Beate has never heard the name.

For the first time in her life she breaks a seal, an oval one with the impression of a bird rising out of the red lump of wax, maybe a Phoenix rising from the ashes. She pulls yellowed handwritten sheets of paper from the envelope. In the slanting light of the round attic windows, she starts to read.

Lüneburg, 8 December 1948

The doctor says I should write everything down. He says the memory is still fresh in my mind. What does he know about it. The day before yesterday he brought me a writing pad. He wants to ask me every day if I've written something. I told him no one would want to read this.

I didn't want to write at first. So the doctor said he would come again in the evening. He said he could move my bed into his surgery. Then we'd be alone. Then I could talk. Frankly. The doctor's nice but I can't talk about it. I'd rather write. Anyway, you can't say what it was like. It was either much worse or completely different. It was just the way it was. I feel as if I'm lying, but I'm not. And it wasn't the same for everyone. Some of the women were stubborn as mules. Some threw themselves at the Russians. Just for a cigarette or bread or something. But most of them were destroyed. Not the worst ones. Here in the Lüneburg Hospital is a lady doctor who knows where I've been. She just says we should forget, as quickly as possible.

It's terribly boring in hospital, but a good bed and nice hot meals. The other women in my room are jealous because three times in between meals I get something to eat. I'm supposed to put on weight. But I don't.

Well then, on 20 January 1945, my sister and I left Hohenneuendorf. Hohenneuendorf is near Bromberg, in West Prussia. Goodness knows what it's called nowadays. My father was killed near Kharkov. My mother didn't want to come with us. She said she'd stay. She sent us away. We thought we'd soon be coming back home. The Führer would never give up the east of Germany. Never.

We had a big cart. The wheels had rubber tyres. Our horses were well fed. We had thick winter coats, fur boots, fur muffs. My sister even had an old-fashioned fur collar of Grandma's. We had jars of dripping, bottled fruit, tea, flour. The most important things were the cigarettes and the schnapps. You could exchange them for anything. So far so good, but so slow, because everyone was leaving. And the snow and ice on the roads. But that was nothing compared to later. We were in one

7

village for nearly three weeks because my sister had
sinusitis. We stayed in a real castle, the people had gone
away. I don't remember what the village was called.

On 27 February, the bay horse couldn't go any
further. We had to find a stable and got to a
Pomeranian village. A farmer took both our horses and
put them in his stable. We gave him schnapps in return.
But the horse was full of snot. The farmer put it out of
its misery. We couldn't stay at the farm. The mayor
said we must go to the vicarage. There were already a lot
of refugees there from the east. A lady curate lived there,
she made room for us. We thought we'd wait there until
our troops started to fight back against the Russians.

The place was called Sageritz. It was a pretty village.
The houses were mostly of green clapboard. The shutters
were painted white. Smoke rose from the chimneys. It
looked very peaceful. Everyone had to dig trenches. My
sister and I too. At first we were alone in the attic room.
Then the lady curate went to Stolp. She wanted to get
money from the bank and buy a pig. People still had
pigs to slaughter. In Stolp she picked up a woman. She
was feverish and confused. She had been looking for her
wounded husband in Stolp, but the military hospital had
already been transferred west. The town hospital was not
taking any more people. So the curate brought the poor
woman back to Sageritz in her cart. The woman slept in
my bed. My sister and I had to share her bed. Up till
then not a shot had been fired in Sageritz.

Bea stops reading Frau Hiller's notes. Stolp. The name

is familiar because her grandmother would often speak of it rapturously, as if it were a little Paris: in Stolp there was an elegant Station Road just as lovely as the Champs-Élysées; Stolpmünde, the Baltic seaside resort, had been her holiday paradise, with its white sand and lovely beech woods.

Bea's father – her grandparents had often spoken of it – had contacted them from a military hospital in Stolp shortly before the end of the war, on 16 February 1945. And there, literally, *his trail disappeared*. Bea knows a good deal more about him, though, because she has the letters he wrote to her mother. She thinks her father the most wistful correspondent, the tenderest sweetheart, writing to his wife: 'Whenever I see you I am a little happier – where will it all lead to? – and also a little unhappier because I know the days of my leave are numbered.' And Bea's mother is the grand lover who, against all reason, ignoring the protests of her parents and friends, still set off in February 1945 to visit her husband in the military hospital in Stolp.

They used to talk about Stolp continually, about her parents, who became *victims of the war* there. It sounded almost comforting, as though her father had gone to sleep in her mother's arms, or she in his. But they never mentioned a place called Sageritz. Bea need only open the manuscript again to read that it was in Sageritz that her mother started to die. Her mother was the pitiful person who was brought in a cart with a pig, from Stolp to Sageritz.

The moment in which she realises this is a split

second between two times, a Copernican shift after which everything will rotate around her mother. As Bea goes down the stairs again, something has changed fundamentally, something which she cannot yet define. 'Shocked to death' is not right. She's still alive, after all, even if the world has started to shake. She goes down the stairs, one step at a time. Behind her in the attic all the junk settles down into a mulch again, abandoned objects restlessly waiting. Bea holds on to the banisters. In her mind's eye is a picture: an icy country road, a cart, a pig and her mother. Going to SAGERITZ. The name is written in block capitals and underlined. *The place was called SAGERITZ. It was a pretty village. Up till then not a shot had been fired in SAGERITZ.*

Bea is going to read the name many more times. When she starts leafing through the notes, dead silverfish fall out from between the pages, and a loose sheet of paper: a short letter addressed to her grandparents, dated 9 May 1948, the paper so brittle and yellow that one has to hold it to the light.

9 May 1948

Dear Herr and Frau Hennig

Four weeks ago I was released from the Magnitogorsk camp. It is my sad duty to be writing to you. On 29 December 1945, your daughter Ruth passed away in the Karabash camp in Siberia. She died without pain, in my arms. You have my deepest sympathy. Your daughter and I were good friends. We exchanged addresses in Konitz, when we knew we were being deported. I learnt your address by heart. I hope it is still right. I am in the Lüneburg Hospital. I survived. Ruth did not. It is not fair.

Yours faithfully,
Hildegard Hiller

There must have been some correspondence after that between Bea's grandfather and Frau Hiller. Knowing her grandfather, he would certainly have wanted to find out more about how his daughter came to be captured and deported. At some point Frau Hiller must have sent Bea's grandfather these pages of her memories, which she had written down on her doctor's recommendations, *while the memory was still fresh*. Grandmother had certainly not been given these pages to read. She was supposed to go on believing that her daughter had died without pain. And Bea was supposed to believe it too. 'We couldn't stop your mother. Just a short while before everything collapsed, she still wanted to go to your father in the Stolp military hospital. And it cost her her life.'

Bea thinks: 'My mother wanted to go to Stolp. No matter what the cost.' Bea thinks: 'My mother *still* wanted to go to Stolp, at that time.'

That little word 'still' is crucial. In view of the Soviet breakthrough in Hinterpommern and the fact that many of the towns in the east of Germany had already been declared fortresses, her decision was sheer madness. With hindsight, it was clearly suicide to do what Bea's mother did. All she can have had in her mind was that the man she loved was lying wounded in hospital. Her family and friends could say what they pleased; Bea's mother packed her suitcase, *an imitation leather suitcase and a green rucksack.* But she could not simply leave: civilians needed a travel permit to use the railway, overloaded as it was with troop transports and wrecked by enemy bombing. The proper authorities to which the young woman had to go, a department of the Deutsche Reichsbahn, had been completely destroyed in the heavy air-raids of 3 February 1945. It took Bea's mother two days, two long, precious days, to find a temporary replacement office somewhere amongst the rubble of the city of Berlin, which had been declared a fortress, and there, thanks to the telegram her husband had sent from hospital, she was indeed issued with a permit to travel to Stolp in Hinterpommern: of course a German soldier's wife can still visit her husband when he's been wounded in action, fighting for the Fatherland! Don't worry, young lady, the Russians won't break through that quickly, you can bank on it, the Führer will rouse himself and lauch a massive assault to win back German land in the east . . . It's *still* early days, all is not lost. *Still, still, still.* The administrative machinery must *still* have been working smoothly. Bea's grandmother prayed that her daughter would be refused the travel permit but her prayers went unheard.

Bea thinks: 'My mother abandoned me, a one-year-old, and ran away towards disaster. No, my mother entrusted me to her mother and said, "I have to go to Stolp." She very nearly took me along as well, to show me to my father: he hadn't seen me yet.'

The young woman must have been panicking. Panicking and great-hearted. This is how Bea imagines her mother: standing in the hall, in a white veil, a myrtle wreath in her thick hair. As she is in the wedding photograph. Or in a housecoat, her hair loose. Or already wearing her warm, fur-lined loden-green coat, with her imitation leather suitcase and rucksack, the message from Stolp in her hand. What would the telegram have said? 'Am in Stolp military hospital stop *Heimatschuss* stop waiting for you . . .' Oh for heaven's sake, he can't really have sent a cable like that. One wasn't allowed to use the word *Heimatschuss* – the lucky bullet which got you sent home – let alone write it down. And that his wife should come and visit him in Stolp, still at that time – the wounded man would surely never have asked that of her. He obviously just wanted to let her know he was still alive. But Bea's mother lost her head and wanted to go to Stolp at once.

It was 26 February 1945.

Bea's relatives used to talk about this black day as if it were the day on which her parents had died. Two weeks after Bea's first birthday, the fateful telegram arrived from her father. Bea imagines the scene taking place in the hall, though it could just as easily have been at the garden gate, or in the kitchen or the living room. She sees the family standing in the hall, on the red-brown tiled floor, light coming through the high window, through the glass bricks; she hears her mother read out the telegram and say, 'I have to go to Stolp'; her grandfather is speechless and her grandmother takes her from her mother's arms and holds her close: 'The child will stay here.'

Did the child cry when Grandfather then started raging at his daughter's folly? He would have told her that she was risking her life travelling to Hinterpommern at that time; the Red Army's offensive couldn't be held back any longer: he listened to the BBC broadcast from London every night and had long since lost any illusions about the outcome of the war.

Later, he used to talk about how he had tried to persuade Bea's mother. 'But we couldn't stop her,' he kept saying, 'alas!'

At that time, Grandfather knew nothing about how at the Yalta Conference in February 1945 Stalin had received the approval of the western powers enabling him to deport a workforce from defeated Germany to the Soviet Union, including women aged between sixteen and thirty-five, as part of the reparations granted to him.

When the Second World War comes up on the lesson plan, Bea shows her class a map of the eastern theatre of war on which the Soviet armies' lines of advance are indicated by black arrows. One of the arrows is pointing directly at Stolp. The pupils have no particular interest in this subject, they don't want to be lectured.

Bea can read on forty yellowed pieces of paper what then commenced, seven kilometres east of Stolp in the village of Sageritz, where it still seemed so peaceful. And she has to read over and over again what Frau Hildegard Hiller wrote, although all the suffering is much more than she can bear.

Russian tanks took Sageritz on 8 March. It was terrible. Shooting, rape, people being taken away. Escape. Confusion. My sister just grabbed our Red Cross bag and we were off. The lady curate said she knew the area. West. Keep going west. It was raining. We pulled the woman who had been staying in the attic on a handcart. And another one with a baby. She had only just given birth. First rest was on a rock under some fir trees. The lady curate had kept her head and had brought bread and dripping, and sausage from the slaughtered pig. She shared it out.

On till evening, still in the woods. Just don't let us meet any Russians. The baby mustn't cry. We walked the whole day. But what's this, the rock again and the fir trees. We had gone in a circle. How could we tell which direction we were going in? We couldn't see the sun, we didn't know where west was. The first night we stayed at a farm. No one was there, just a goat. We milked it and drank the warm milk. In the kitchen there were still embers glowing in the stove. The larder was full. We ate. We slept in freshly made-up beds. And then a big breakfast, like in peacetime. Then we risked walking along the road. Just not in a circle again.

I still remember, there were birch trees all along the road. Little pieces of ice fell from them. We covered up the women and the baby. Then a herd of pigs came running towards us. We arrived at a place called QUAKENBURG. *Then four Russians came along the road, on bicycles. They kept riding round and round us, shouting, 'Davay! Davay!' Then they chased us into a house. There were a lot of women and children there already. We were divided up. Children taken from their mothers. So much crying. People with the same surname were separated. No one could stay together. My sister had to go to another house. I wanted to go with her of course, but the soldiers forced me back. We had no choice.*

The next morning I couldn't find my sister. That was the worst thing. Then we had to line up and be counted. Counted over and over again. Being counted in Russian is provertje. *An interpreter told us we would just be part of a labour force. We even believed him. We were split up into columns. Each column had thirty-three women. One woman had to be the overseer. The interpreter asked who wanted to be the overseer. Several women volunteered at once.*

Then on through ice and snow. By Shanks' pony, you'd call it. First to KRÜSSEN. *Then to* BALDENBURG. *Thirty-five kilometres a day. I could see that on the signposts, how far it was. Nights in coal cellars. In prisons, on cement floors. More and more captured women joined us.*

In Baldenburg we had to leave the handcarts behind.
That was when Frau Wischnewsky arrived. She knew a
little Polish. She just went and got the carts again, even
though the Russians shouted at her. Frau Wischnewsky
said, 'Woman baby and woman kaput.' And that they
couldn't walk. Then the soldiers let the woman with the
baby go. They said, 'Damoy,' which means go home.
But the woman couldn't really walk. She can't have
managed to get home. The other woman had to come
with us, no matter how. When she couldn't walk any
more she was hit with a rifle butt, behind the knees.

Underneath these words there is a picture of a rifle
placed down on a surface, the fine lines drawn very
precisely, showing the butt and the lock, the long
barrel and a strap.

In the days which follow, Bea leaves everything,
makes a copy of the forty crumbling pages and types
them out. The small, old-fashioned handwriting is
hard to decipher. Some of the sentences are completely or partially crossed out: even with the paper
held up to the light one can only guess what it was
that no one was intended to read. Names of places are
written carefully in block capitals: STOLP, SAGER-
ITZ, QUAKENBURG, KRÜSSEN, BALDEN-
BURG, RUMMELSBURG, KONITZ, SOLDAU,
KORKINO, KOPEISK, KARABASH. Standing out
of the text like this, the names create a litany which

Bea recites over and over, though she has never been to any of these places. STOLP, SAGERITZ, QUA-KENBURG, KRÜSSEN, BALDENBURG, RUM-MELSBURG, KONITZ, SOLDAU, KORKINO, KOPEISK, KARABASH.

She searches maps for the names. The Pomeranian names of the German places are only to be found in an old school atlas of her mother's. SAGERITZ, QUAKENBURG. There she has to trace the path for a circular walk. Her hand shakes while she draws the line. *But what's this? We had walked in a circle.* You have to go west. Keep going west. *We didn't know where west was.* On from QUAKENBURG to KRÜSSEN, from KRÜSSEN to BALDENBURG and on further to RUMMELSBURG and to KONITZ. Konitz is in what used to be West Prussia and now has the Polish name Chojnice. Frau Hiller writes that in Konitz the women finally understood that they had been deported.

On the farm in Konitz almost all of us were raped. They just shouted 'woman come'. Some had to go four or five times. I did twice. You can't write down how awful it was. And no one would be interested either. One of them shoved me into a stable. I couldn't do anything. He ripped my clothes off. He put his pistol down on my chest. Pointing towards my chin. He held the pistol with one hand. Otherwise I would have shot him. Or myself. I hadn't ever been with a man. I couldn't do anything. Just keep still. When he was

18

finished he took my winter coat.

Ruth's green coat was gone as well. She hadn't undressed quickly enough. So one of them slit her clothes with his bayonet. He cut her on her breast while he was doing it. When it was all finished we had to line up. We stood there in our rags like gypsies as if we didn't really exist any more. I kept having to think of my sister, whether the same had happened to her. Because she was only fifteen. Ruth could hardly stand. She was bleeding so much. They shut us up for the night in a pig sty. Eight women to each sty. I can't think about it any more. At least they didn't get anyone out again. Ruth and I (the latter part of the sentence is crossed out).

Bea's mother was no longer 'the woman who had been staying in the attic', or 'the pitiful person'. Now she was called Ruth. And Frau Hiller seems to have thought of her as a substitute for her missing sister. She writes that on the following morning the women were allowed to loot the wardrobes of the farmhouse and that she was able to get hold of the warmest things for herself and Bea's mother. They all looked like *people in a play*.

When they had to line up again in groups at Konitz railway station before getting on the train, Frau Wischnewsky said while she was counting them that thirty-three wasn't the right number any more: there were probably already a few more, you just couldn't see it yet. In one group a woman was missing. So all the women were herded back to the farm and told that if the missing woman was not found they would all be shot. They did find her, in the park: half frozen to death, she lay there with her legs spread, a very young girl, and one of the soldiers shoved a pine cone into her vagina. *We had to leave her there*, writes Frau Hiller, and: *All Russians are animals.*

It was of course inconceivable for most Germans at that time that they had brought this hell upon themselves. Bea wonders whether her mother was capable of understanding the historical context. Would knowledge like that have been of any help to her, as flight turned into captivity, and captivity into deportation? Would the rape have been less terrible if she had understood it as an act of vengeance?

Bea mustn't read Frau Hiller's notes too often. She should really hide the pages from herself, otherwise who knows how they will change her life, what feelings they will stir up. She already has dreams in which she is crawling along sloping boards, running towards doors while her feet refuse to move from the spot.

What would have happened if her grandfather had told her when she was younger about her mother's fate, if she had found out more than just *missing, presumed dead at end of war*, and in Stolp *his trail disappeared*. If, instead of these meaningless clichés, words like captivity, deportation and labour camp had been used, could Bea have painted her mother's picture between them?

Suddenly she is able to read about something that

happened to countless women in the last weeks of the war. A Frau Hildegard Hiller from Hohenneuendorf, near Bromberg, became the victims' biographer, their unwilling chronicler, taking up her pen on doctor's orders after her return home. And now Bea has it in black and white, what happened to her mother.

She used to think very little about her mother. She was simply a war orphan. Many of her contemporaries had lost their fathers and mothers, and only rarely does it occur to children that circumstances could be other than the way they are. In the graveyard which Bea can see from the attic window – a French garden divided by severely pruned hedges into numerous squares and rectangles – there was no grave for her mother, one which she could have looked after, and she had no memories apart from the one she never really had, from 26 February 1945. Bea has conjured this farewell scene so powerfully in her imagination that it has become a perpetual *déjà vu*, a recurring familiar image acted out in front of the coloured glass bricks of the hall window.

As a child she used to put 'grand' in front of the word 'mother', and only occasionally thought that her real mother would probably have been less strict than her grandmother. Later, the woman who had given birth to her and then shortly after, blinded by love, set off for Stolp, came to seem to her a tragic heroine, a Juliet, an Ophelia, an Isolde, a distant, heroic figure she almost envied, whose love had cost her her life.

Yet now, the *she paid for it with her life* is no longer merely a dramatic phrase, it is the naked truth. Now a soldier hits Bea's mother behind the knees with his rifle butt. Now another slashes her coat with his bayonet and attacks her. And Bea finds herself thinking: 'In which world did she put her coat on and in which did a bayonet slash it?' Bea ought to be able to see it as an act of revenge but she just sees her mother crouching in a coal cellar, in a stinking pig sty, pulling a German helmet out of a looted mass grave beside the railway embankment, to use for cooking or as a chamber pot. A woman who is raging and who cannot grasp what has happened to her.

Frau Bandilla wasn't fooled. In Soldau she said, 'God protect us, we're being deported.' When she said that about being deported, Ruth started laying into her. She started hammering with both fists against Frau Bandilla's chest and shouting, 'That's not true, that's not true.'
Frau Bandilla had a sister. She was called Frau Piaken. In Quakenburg the Russians hadn't noticed they were sisters. So they could stay together. I was very jealous of them. They came from Masuren and hadn't managed to escape.
Frau Piaken was crafty. In Krüssen they deloused us for the first time. We all had to strip naked. We had to keep walking round and round in a circle. They searched all our things. You couldn't hide anything. But Frau Piaken still hid her watch. I don't know where but I can guess.
At some station or other she noticed on the clock that it was Russian time. We had all been locked in the

station till the next loading. So Frau Piaken changed the time on her watch, that is two hours forwards. Ruth saw her do it and it scared her. She slapped Frau Piaken round the face and shouted, 'Don't drive us all mad,' as if Frau Piaken could do anything about it, that it was Russian time now. The guard separated them, he was shouting, 'Pochemu?' which means why. He kept yelling. Frau Wischnewsky said he was shouting 'Whore with the Mother of God!' and that it was the worst Russian curse.

I'd just like to know why I'm writing all this down. Nobody wants to read it anyway. Definitely not the doctor either, he just wants to keep me busy here. He treats me like a child. He keeps asking, 'Have we been good and written something yet today?'

Bea's grandfather kept Frau Hiller's notes well hidden. Why did he not destroy them, or, if he wanted Bea to read them at a later date, store them at a friend's house? Did his life change after he learned the fate of his only daughter? Did he too have to turn the pages compulsively, reading what happened in Stolp, in Sageritz, in Krüssen, in Baldenburg, Rummelsburg, Konitz, in Soldau and then in Korkino, Kopeisk and Karabash?

Grandfather was almost blind in his last years, but he would certainly have known the content of these pages off by heart. Like his psalms, which he recited without moving his lips: 'I am weary of my crying: my throat is dried.' He could not talk to anyone about what he had read, no more than Frau Hiller, amongst the last to be repatriated, could talk about her experiences. On almost every page she complains about having to stay silent, always using the same words: *Nobody wants to know about it anyway*.

You can't talk about it to anyone. Bea's tongue sticks to the roof of her mouth too. Who wants to hear about deported women nowadays? If you want to talk about that sort of thing you come up against complete lack of interest or disbelief. Other people's complaints are irritating. What happened years ago is not today's topic. Bea tried once to talk to a colleague about it, but she could think of nothing better to say than, 'I should forget all about it as quickly as possible.' Until the unification of Germany this woman lived in Magdeburg and she knows that in the former East Germany one was not allowed to use the words 'deportation' or 'rape' – to do so was to risk a prison sentence.

And historians haven't put on record what happened either, that three or four hundred thousand women, or whatever the exact number was, were deported. No monument to these women was erected, no history book records their abduction. Bea wonders whether, as the clock struck Russian time, the captive women still heard any news about world events. Frau Hiller writes almost nothing about it. Banal objects – a blanket, a spoon or a comb – were more important than the greater picture. It was as though the abducted women had disappeared from the world. Timeless in no man's land.

Only once does she mention that they heard rumours that Russian and American forces had joined up at the River Elbe, that Germany was being divided into two countries and that Hitler was dead. From her distant perspective, the reports of Germany's collapse and the Führer's death must have seemed like malicious slander. She writes: *But nothing could make me believe it.*

Bea should put the notes away, she shouldn't be struggling with memories that are not her own. She must not become obsessed with the idea of her mother's extraordinary resurrection from her mass grave in Siberia. Had she been confronted with all the facts earlier she would probably have digested them, as one says, long ago. The discovery in the attic caught her unawares. The slightest thing is enough to trigger off images which she does not wish to see. She just has to sit on her bicycle and four Russian soldiers surround her. She cannot even put on her coat without thinking about her mother's loden-green, fur-lined one. How can one stop the pictures juxtaposing themselves? Lately she has avoided travelling by S-Bahn. The rhythmic sound of the wheels suddenly transports her into a goods train, rolling eastwards, day after day, week after week. Through the single barred window one can see the empty countryside, untilled fields, woods ravaged by fire, charred earth. When the train brakes, the women fall towards the engine, one on top of another. The shrieking brakes, the opening and closing of the sliding door. The noise of the iron bolts. The '*davay,*

davay!' The *'provertje'*. One, two, three. Shouted from behind them in Russian, *'Ras, dva, tri.'*

Frau Hiller describes it all very vividly. Sometimes, not every day, a bucket of hot food was shoved into their train carriage, cabbage soup, beetroot soup, potato soup. Often there was just dry bread and water. Bread and water do not multiply, *the lady curate could pray for it to happen till she was blue in the face.* Frau Hiller detested the lady curate's prayers. Her Führer would allow no other gods before him.

In some places the text is broken up with pictures which are easier to make out than the faded handwriting: little lines of goods trucks, huts, steel helmets, pistols, shorn plaits of hair, crosses, arrows, Soviet stars, the hammer and sickle. One page is completely framed by a tangle of shapes which looks like barbed wire, but it is supposed to be Russian thistles, or tumbleweed, which the writer calls 'witch of the steppes', and she describes how the stuff was blown over the gravel of a stretch of the railway line in Siberia.

It must have been around the end of August. We were taken from Korkino to Kopeisk. The train kept stopping, and children dressed in rags threw stones at us. We were allowed to go to the toilet more often because most of us had diarrhoea. Some couldn't even get down from the train. We made them sit on the bucket. You can't imagine the smell in the heat. Ruth got out of the train with me. She sat down straight away, half under the train. It still embarrassed her so much. Then she quickly

came back, because under the train was such a noise.
Eerie. It was really piercing. It came from the witch of
the steppes. The wind was chasing it furiously over the
rails and all around underneath the train.

Our shorn hair had already grown back. Ruth's too.
The yellow stuff from the thistles had got caught in her
hair. Later on I picked it out properly. In Korkino we
had washed our hair in our urine and rinsed it in
saltwater. That had helped against the lice but afterwards
it stung a lot. You could scratch till it bled. Instead of
hair we had very clean straw on our heads. It rustled
loudly.

Bea is haunted by the 'witch of the steppes'. A few
days after finding the notes, she takes her class of
sixteen-year-olds to the Hamburger Bahnhof, the
museum of modern art, to an exhibition called
'Routes to Berlin', which is being shown as part of
the celebration of the city's 750th anniversary. The
schoolchildren care very little about the different
routes to Berlin, by water, land and air, or about the
design of the Berlin railway stations. They want to see
the veteran cars, the legendary Silver Arrow on the
Avus; the BMW Dixi and Bernd Rosemeier in an
Auto Union car; the Schienenzeppelin, which could
achieve the ridiculous maximum speed of a hundred
and eighty kilometres an hour; flying machines held
together with wire and paddle steamers dating back to
the year dot, and maybe even nostalgic blue sleeping
cars, dining cars and Pullman carriages.

Bea stands for a long time in front of one photograph which shows a goods train, a plank slanting in through the open sliding door. Clumps of yellow prickly saltwort grow rampant between the rails. In the close-up photograph one can see the twigs branching out and how tightly they have become entangled into little balls. Underneath the picture it says: *Grunewald Station – Transportation of Berlin Jews, 1943.*

'So that's where they went from,' says a soft man's voice close behind Bea. The voice belongs to a man who is looking at the pictures with Bea's colleague Doctor Kurz. Bea should have listened to her heart and followed that voice, then she and Jacob would have begun their story a few years earlier.

But who listens to their heart? Bea listens to the noise that her pupils are making. They are her responsibility.

'So that's where they went from,' are the first words that Bea hears Jacob speak, and she thinks of them each time she goes up or down the hill to the Grunewald S-Bahn station, past the long stretch of concrete wall with the impressions of human bodies on it.

How high is the probability, in a city of four million inhabitants like Berlin, of running into someone a second time? When Doctor Kurz introduces Jacob to Bea five years later, she thinks that it could only have happened because she was waiting for it to happen. She did not forget his voice. The *So that's where they went from*.

The day on which Bea meets Jacob again. A school day like any other. One would never survive the morning without break-time. Smoking has recently been prohibited in the staff room. Anyone who *has* to smoke should kindly go to the kitchenette which has officially been declared the smokehouse. Bea doesn't have to smoke but she likes to stand at the open window of the smokehouse as it is more peaceful there than in the staff room. Behind her a voice says, 'Are you one of the smokers now?' The voice belongs to Doctor Kurz. He teaches biology, English, and Russian as an optional subject, and is considered by the other staff to be arrogant and taciturn. Nevertheless he now asks Bea if she would like to accompany him that evening to an international symposium of the Amcha Foundation.

Bea has no idea what the Amcha Foundation is and only starts to take notice when he tells her that the theme of the conference will be the survivors of the Holocaust; how almost all of them are condemned to silence because no one wants to listen to the terrible things they have to tell. And how all that they suffered during their persecution is made far worse through having to keep silent about it now.

Bea has never been anywhere with Doctor Kurz off the school premises, apart from on staff outings where Kurz, if he takes part in them at all, prefers to keep himself shrouded in his cigar smoke.

So, now he is inviting Bea to go with him to a symposium of the Amcha Foundation and she accepts, because she has nothing better planned. Or does she accept because she hopes to meet the man whom Kurz was with at the exhibition at the Hamburger Bahnhof museum? Or is it because she thinks that it may be possible at a convention of this kind to focus the discussion on other people who are condemned to silence too, for instance on the women who were deported to the Soviet Union?

Before the conference even starts she has lost her

nerve to speak at it. Can one victim be compared to another? The Jews, who definitely were not Germany's war enemies, with the German women who were seized as reparation along with railway tracks, carriages and industrial equipment, their labour intended to compensate for the losses and suffering Germany had caused in enemy territory? The spotlight of history has not fallen on these victims. The unheard-of things that happened remain, literally, unheard. No traces were left behind, no mountains of shoes, spectacles, dentures, hair. Perhaps Bea would be able to clarify the differences between the victims, between the industrial mass extermination of those who died during the war and the wretched deaths of the others afterwards, but, she thinks, when one of us starts talking, it can easily sound as if we're trying to justify ourselves, or to argue that victims should be differentiated into first and second class.

Next to Bea sits an engaging and enthusiastic young Levite Jew who is talking to the old Jewish lady sitting in front of him about the kosher slaughter of animals, kosher cookery and wine. The old lady turns her head to him and admits that she has converted to Christianity, she did it out of deep conviction, for Jesus of Nazareth was the first Jew to free himself from the demonic dietary laws. A children's choir sings plaintive Yiddish songs. The large hall is full to bursting. Young people are sitting on the window sills and crouching on the steps that lead to the podium. Papers are presented, addressing the issue of how almost all survivors stay silent because they cannot find the language for their suffering, they are unable to speak the unspeakable; and this crippling silence, says one speaker, who has somehow escaped from it himself, can even lead to post-traumatic stress in the next generation, to behavioural problems, insecurity and mistrust, children going through their parents' experience of being persecuted as though they were victims themselves. This next generation could, he says, be called the seventh million.

A Dutch neurologist gives a detailed description of the symptoms which are caused by unspoken fears, and gives the names of organisations to which sufferers can come for help. Doctor Kurz makes a note of the addresses of advice centres offering group therapy and individual counselling. The speaker says that this reticence can affect not only the victims and their children but also the perpetrators: the murder of the Jewish people had only been possible under a cloak of secrecy. Efforts to start a dialogue between the victims, or the survivors, and the perpetrators, had quite understandably so far hardly ever been successful.

As they leave the lecture theatre, Bea's colleague says that he has arranged to meet a university friend here. He was definitely supposed to come but sadly doesn't seem to have turned up. It's a pity, a great pity. It is a long time since they last met, and he's been looking forward to seeing him again. They wait around in the cloakroom until all the coats and hats have been collected, but the friend seems really not to have been there. Only later, in the dimly lit car park, he appears, saying, 'Here I am at last! Can you forgive me?' Bea's colleague stretches his arms out wide and cries, 'This is just typical of you! Where on earth have you been?' and turning to Bea, 'So, now we have him! This is Jacob Stern. I studied botany with him, but he's gone on to great things. I'm sure a flower's already been named after him!'

Bea names a flower after him very soon. Jacob asks his friend for her address and then 'says it with flowers'. He sends a bouquet of purple, white and yellow stock; it is fragrant and tells her what Jacob will later express as: 'You were a stroke of luck for me,' or, 'You crossed my path at exactly the right moment,' adding, 'Or what do you want to hear?'

What does Bea want to hear? What does she want to hear from the very beginning? Something similar to what her father, a lance-corporal of the Wehrmacht, wrote with numb fingers to her mother as he sat in a bullet- and shatter-proof dugout near Leningrad: 'I would be desperate here if you, my dearest, were not by me and keeping me warm.'

Bea ought to understand right away that one cannot measure her relationship with Jacob against her legendary parents' brief marriage. Bea hates the word 'relationship'. A colleague of hers loves to give detailed descriptions of the partners she has had during her various 'life phases'. Once she even rented a man by the hour, really rented him, for a fee. One can do that nowadays. She went out with him, danced with him, slept with him and said she found the relationship quite satisfactory, dismissing him again when she found another one for whom she did not need to pay.

A single woman like Bea – without kith or kin, as the colleague says – must be careful. That sort of person tends to be particularly susceptible to a man's stammered declarations of love.

Jacob does not stammer any declarations of love. Jacob sends flowers and invites Bea out to dinner. When they are sitting opposite one another in a restaurant for the first time, Bea finds out nothing about him at all except that he used to go wandering around in jungles, in almost virgin forest – as they still are in New Zealand and on the Seychelles – places where one holds one's breath, the silence is so overwhelming, where one only looks upwards because most of the plants don't grow on the forest floor, they flourish high up in the tree-tops – but these plants aren't parasitic, they are called epiphytes, they literally live off air and filter everything else they need from the rain. Bea has trouble imagining the well-groomed, portly Doctor Stern in the jungle, but she feigns enormous interest in the virgin forest of New Zealand and the Seychelles, and by the end of the meal is nearly in tears as her companion gives a graphic account of the imminent destruction of the earth's gigantic green lungs; he describes the burning of forest and the inferno of the widespread fires as though his own home were in peril. Helping her into her coat as they leave the restaurant, Doctor Stern says softly into her ear that he thinks it absolutely charming of her to be such a patient listener.

In the weeks that follow, Jacob brings his flowers himself and lets Bea cook for him. Days go by when she hears nothing. And then suddenly he will arrive at her door unexpectedly, a surprise guest.

When Bea's hair is unwashed or she is in a housecoat without her make-up on, she pretends she is not at home, stands at the closed door and watches Jacob through the spy hole: his face is always differently distorted, depending on whether it comes up close to the little lens or moves away. These are images which offend the eye; Bea dare not breathe and is quite unable to turn the key and stand there in front of him, caught unawares like this. That was something she could have afforded to do only in her younger years.

Yet she would so love to let him in and kiss his feeble excuses away – 'Just popping in,' 'May I?', 'Disturbing you?', 'Gone in a moment'. She doesn't want to let him go away again. He stands at her front door, from head to toe one big cry for help: *I would be desperate here if you were not by me and keeping me warm*. Jacob would sooner bite his tongue off than say such a thing. He lays his bouquet of stock, his 'Jacob's flowers', on the doormat, goes away and telephones her to arrange a time to meet. She should be happy that he is no longer as shy with her as in the first weeks of their acquaintance; after all, they have managed to progress from the formal '*Sie*' to '*du*' and from kissing the hand to kissing the cheeks. They must be the most awkward couple in Berlin. Once bitten, twice shy?

The colleague through whom Bea met Jacob, Kurz, mentioned once that Jacob got married when he was a student. She was a dark beauty, but right from the start the marriage was doomed: his friend was simply a loner, or did he say lone wolf? 'If you ask me,' said Doctor Kurz, looking Bea over rather audaciously, 'if you ask me, our friend Jacob has already made quite a few women unhappy. There's something about him which women are taken in by, but all those who wanted to marry him were very quickly shown the door.'

Bea did not like the tone he adopted when he talked about Jacob, she didn't like the 'our friend Jacob', nor the 'taken in by'. Kurz talked about him as though his friend were somebody notorious. Nevertheless, Bea sometimes sounds him out since he is the only person who can tell her anything about Jacob. His answers always start with, 'If you ask me,' or 'As far as I know . . .'

'If you ask me, Jacob never thinks about his father. He seems to have been completely assimilated. As far as I know, Jacob blames his father for not leaving Berlin in time and for bringing disaster on his mother.'

Deliberately casually, Bea enquires whether Jacob has any children.

'Children? Not that I know of,' replies her colleague. 'I can't really imagine that Jacob would have brought children into a world in which he doesn't like living. He's always so merciless in his

36

diagnosis of the causes of our misery. Even as a student he liked to quote Brecht: "Truly, I'm living in dark times! The happy man just hasn't heard the terrible news yet." Please, see if you can cheer him up a bit.'

Bea needs cheering up herself, but she will try to cheer Jacob up. It is not easy. Music which she finds soothing makes Jacob melancholy. He calls theatre productions 'one electric shock after another' to which he does not wish to expose himself. Bea loves riding her bicycle, rides it for kilometres along the old border between east and west or in the Grunewald. Jacob claims never to have sat on a bicycle voluntarily; as far as he is concerned it need never have been invented. Anyway, he has back problems. If he had not told her himself, Bea would never have believed that when he was younger he had gone on daring expeditions through tropical forests: it must have been quite some time ago. Nowadays one can barely even get him to go for a stroll. Bea adores swimming, in the summer she swims in all the accessible lakes in the area, in winter in indoor pools; free of her own weight, she revels in an element that supports her, she turns on her back, lets herself drift, comes home thoroughly exhausted and relaxed. Jacob shudders at the mere thought of having to get into the water. So, there is no point in saying, 'Swim away from your sadness, get on a bicycle, cycle along the old "Death Strip". If you don't like the word sport, call it therapy.'

Instead, they drive out by car into the environs of Berlin which are accessible once more, as far as the

Spreewald, to Wipersdorf, to the quiet, unspoilt countryside of Fläming. And of course one day they go to Potsdam, to the palace of Sanssouci. When they are told to put on big grey slippers to protect the valuable floors, Jacob refuses, saying he wouldn't be able to walk a step in the things, he will go to the Orangerie in the meantime. So then Bea doesn't want to visit the palace any more either. She takes the slippers off again and goes with Jacob. A peacock struts around in front of them and fans out its tail. Then it gives a hideous scream. Now Jacob doesn't want to go into the Orangerie either. He doesn't want to go anywhere. He wants to return home at once. He is disgruntled; once again, their outing has turned out differently from what she had planned.

Most of their outings turn out differently from what she has planned. In their first summer together they explore Mark Brandenburg, two Berliners who can at last come out from behind the Wall. One day they follow the footsteps of the writer Fontane to the village of Stechlin, and to Lake Stechlin, of which old Dubslav was so proud. These enchanted waters were supposed to have a mysterious connection with the greater movements of the earth: whenever there was an earthquake, or a volcano erupted somewhere, a jet of water would shoot up into the air from the middle of the lake.

Jacob knows all this, of course, and the only thing he says about old Dubslav is to point out that Fontane made the livelihood of the great landowner dependent on a Jewish creditor; even in Fontane one finds hidden anti-Semitism.

Before them is the lake, mysterious, 'like a mute, who feels moved to speak but whose captive tongue refuses to serve him, and what he wants to say remains unsaid'.

Like a turquoise flash, a kingfisher skims close to the surface of the water, calling its shrill 'zii-ti'. Bea wants to get into the lake and swim, and encourages Jacob to bathe too, but he shudders at the thought, as though just at that very moment a huge plume of water had shot out of the lake and announced an earthquake, a volcano, a forest fire which can never be extinguished, or some other even worse catastrophe.

Bea cannot help laughing. She goes behind a clump of reeds and wades stark naked into the lake. She swims front crawl into the middle of the lake, flings herself onto her back and kicks fountains up into the air, higher and higher, until it looks as if the water plume is announcing the end of the world. Treading water, she watches Jacob sit down on a rotten tree trunk which is lying on the shore. If she were to sit down next to him, he would poke a stick between the halves of the trunk and give her a schoolmasterish lecture on the fungi and centipedes which make good use of the mulch. To hell with botany, when Jacob hides himself from her in forests and rotten tree trunks.

He's going back to the car now, hesitantly. It looks as though he's dragging his right leg behind him. If he had a driving licence, he'd probably drive off, his feelings hurt, and leave her behind in Lake Stechlin.

One weekend, Bea travels to Cracow with her class of eighteen-year-olds. In the city centre they come out onto Skawinzka Street, in the old Jewish quarter, Kazimierz, from where seventy thousand Jews were expelled, and they cannot believe their eyes: above one of the doorways is a Star of David, and walking along the street towards them comes a member of the SS, in the flesh, wearing a black uniform with the SS insignia and the Death's Head on the collar, and a peaked cap. Is he a ghost? He grins at them, raises his arm in a salute and cheerily calls out hello in English. He is, as they then hear, an extra in *Schindler's List*, which Steven Spielberg is currently filming.

On her return from Cracow, Bea tells Jacob about the shock she had, but he just becomes irritated and says that he certainly won't be going to see the film: what happened during that time wasn't something to make into a play or act out. Producers stop at nothing; come hell or high water they'll film it – Lights, camera, action! Scene One, Grunewald Station, loading of last Berlin Jews; Scene Two, everyone has to take their clothes off before they . . . There are even jigsaw puzzles now where you have to piece together whole concentration camps – which skull belongs to which neck, which plait to which head? And in France – this Jacob has seen with his own eyes – you can buy comics about Auschwitz: in the speech bubbles are the sentries' commands and the cries of the victims . . . He, Jacob, wouldn't be surprised if they staged an Auschwitz musical on Broadway next, like the one about the sinking of the Titanic, completely lifelike, deathlike, the salvaged ship's bell ringing and some clever chef offering cookery books with recipes from the galley . . .

Bea objects, saying that a film like *Schindler's List* is important for her older pupils. In the history lesson she'd even recommend that they see it, for experience shows that films, like exhibitions, offer the best opportunity to force young people out of their apathy and indifference. There are educational films too, which include clips of television newsreels from the Nazi era, with marching, Reich's party conferences, Hitler's and Goebbels' speeches. That's how subsequent generations can see for themselves how people in totalitarian countries become intoxicated, and it's the best way to warn young people against blind enthusiasm –

'Or to make them enthusiastic all over again! Have you ever asked yourself whether your lessons about German history sanitise rather than reveal?' Jacob looks at Bea as if he would like to add, 'And what do you know about it, anyway?'

★

What does she know about it, anyway?

Bea has known for a few years that her mother was deported and raped, did forced labour in Siberia and died horribly in the Karabash labour camp. Bea knows that the women there all had to work like slaves and that they were all hungry and all had the same will to live, but Bea knows that her mother did not build herself a dubious career there as a brigade leader. Bea knows that her mother built a snowman there, for her. Bea knows that her father was a very private man and hated all military lingo, but that he nevertheless took part in the siege of Leningrad. And Bea thinks that she knows that her grandparents were not party members but also that they had not dared to oppose the criminal machinations of the dictator, if indeed they knew what was going on. Was their abstention really participation? What does she know about it? Bea knows that she would have no consistent answers ready, if Jacob were to question her.

Since Jacob stepped into her life in that dark car park, she has not been reading Frau Hiller's notes so compulsively, nor her father's letters to her mother. But she would like to tell Jacob about them – Jacob, who is well on the way to driving her mad. Why does he shut himself off from her like this?

For one whole summer he is simply her admirer, her beau; he brings her flowers, kisses her hand, at the very most her cheek, sits at her table and browses through her books. Bea thinks: 'We're united by a sort of clumsy familiarity. I'm only seducing him in my thoughts, just in my thoughts. Why on earth do we try to hide how fond we are of each other?'

Bea, at least, wants more than friendship, even if it means losing her independence. This year she does not make any plans for her summer holidays. She fervently hopes that Jacob and she will go away somewhere together, anywhere. Even if it were to the remotest forest and she were to fall into the clutches of a fully grown boa constrictor. But though Jacob talks a lot about his travels around the world, he contents himself now with day trips, bouquets of flowers and kisses on the cheek. Does he want to serve Bea for seven years, like his biblical namesake? He has obviously never learnt to express his feelings. Just once, as they are walking along the Teltow Canal, he casually remarks that Bea crossed his path just at the right time, a stroke of luck ... and then he immediately applies his intellectual coolness again, the way she applies her make-up, and pokes around with his walking stick on the river bank. Instead of further declarations, she has to listen to some valuable information about the level of the water in the canal and the water table and the gradient of the shore. When they lean far out over the river bank, their reflections tremble on the water.

Even on that day Bea is unable to break down Jacob's reserve and disconcert him.

When she invites him into the house, the first thing he does is to ask if he can please close all the doors and windows. He can only breathe in closed rooms, a quirk left over from childhood.

Bea cooks him delicious meals, but he is usually so deeply sunk in thought that he does not notice what he is eating, has no idea how long she stood in the kitchen getting it all ready. When she asks him what his favourite meal is, he shakes his head as if he does not know the words: 'Favourite meal?' He sits there, smokes his beloved pipe and looks at Bea forlornly. She cannot say, 'What your mother used to cook for you because you liked it best of all.' She just tells him that her favourite dish is called 'Heaven and Earth', and that her grandmother used to conjure it up out of potatoes and apples even in the lean times after the war. She will serve 'Heaven and Earth' next time.

The next time does not happen, because Jacob, as he tells her on the telephone, has to have a hip operation. It has been causing him pain for a long time; he has been hiding it from her. But please, no hospital visits, it's quite enough that all the doctors and nurses will stand around his bed fiddling, he hopes she understands and he'll be in touch when it's all over and he's fit again.

Is it all over, before it has even begun? Is Doctor Stern discreetly withdrawing from the affair? Will Bea have to struggle along on her own again now? Should she go off somewhere on holiday anyway? Or should she sit here and wait for the telephone to whimper?

She should start doing all the things she used to do again. How could she have managed to go for so many months without bicycle rides and swimming? She must practise as she preaches and kick away her gloom, swim away from her sadness and go for a walk along the Teltow Canal. But she cannot bring herself to leave her house and her garden. After all, the telephone could ring and Jacob's perpetually husky voice could say what her father wrote to her mother: *Saying goodbye is always so dreadful . . . The first days after our parting are always the worst.*

Bea lies in the swing hammock between blossoming dahlias and fading stock. No one can see her behind the fence where the hops grow thickest. There are mauve catchfly plants by the small pond, and a green-and-brown-striped dragonfly shoots over the surface of the water. A yellow, red and gold peacock butterfly settles for a moment on the armrest of the hammock and looks at her out of its large counterfeit eyes, the edges of its wings trembling. Last night Bea dreamed that Jacob gave her a big book to read and dead silverfish fell out from between the pages. He had written down for her how he had managed to survive the war. He hugged her so hard that it hurt, and said the tenderest things. But even in the dream she knew it was just a dream.

The hope that Jacob will come back to her lies in her path like a trap. She must not walk into it, must not confuse fiction with reality. Her disappointment would be too great, if what she longs for comes to nothing. It would be better to get used to the idea that Jacob has gone. His forest has swallowed him up. A carnivorous plant has swallowed him up. A catastrophe. But Lake Stechlin isn't foaming.

Was it nothing more than an 'unsuccessful relationship' then? Just because someone is called Jacob and has a beautiful mouth and such dark eyes which have never learned to laugh, doesn't mean it has to be love. Bea would do better carefully to consider how she can escape without being hurt too badly; she should take things less seriously. Yet a part of her has got left behind in that dark car park, and a familiar voice says, *Here I am at last! Can you forgive me?*

Perhaps it would help Bea to get over it if she were to talk to someone openly about her lovesickness. Would she find the right words? She would only be able to describe how it all began, how she saw Jacob for the first time in the museum, heard his voice for the first time – *So that's where they went from* – and how she had met him again years later. *So, now we have him! This is Jacob Stern.* Then, one thing at a time, it would all be described: the 'Jacob's flowers', the kisses on the hand and the cheek, the walks through Mark Brandenburg, the delicious meals she prepared for Jacob . . . And then how Doctor Stern, under the pretext of not wishing to receive visitors in hospital, thought fit simply to disappear.

Bea gives way to her tears. It's time to come back to herself again, in the truest sense of the words. She must finally come back to herself again. Her house must be her home again, even without Jacob. She cannot bear his reserve, his cynicism. He never once invited her to his house. She doesn't know his full address. He only mentioned Lichterfelde. Lichterfelde Süd? Lichterfelde West? She has no idea. What does he want from her? This man is someone who casts shadows without standing in the light. Sends flowers and lectures her. Lets her drive him around. Wants to visit Schloss Sanssouci and turns back at the entrance. Makes her compliments and eats her food up. And that was it. Basically she should be furious with him.

Bea gets Frau Hiller's notes out again. On repeated readings the text changes. Between the lines she can now see how laboriously one word after another was set down on paper, how slight the hope that someone would want to hear them. The deleted sentences, which are almost impossible to decipher, become more eloquent than those she can read.

Bea turns the pages over and then back again, and suffers, as though she could replace her self-pity with the pity she feels for her mother, or as though one pain could diminish the other.

The neighbours are having a party in the garden. Smoke from the grill fills her nostrils. Over her head, beneath the canopy of the swing hammock, floats a cloud of gnats. Is today 30 August?

On 30 August we arrived in Kopeisk. A small camp. Two huts for the women, huts for the kitchens, sick huts. A wash-house, a few shacks. No furniture. We slept there on the hot wooden floor. Over thirty degrees in the shade. And then at night there were seachlights, the whole camp was lit up. As though anyone could have escaped. Where to? Once a woman really did run away, just like that. A guard brought her back. We all had to line up. The woman had to take her shoes off. Two others had to hold her. Then the guard beat her on the heels, with a stick.

The mosquitoes were worst in Kopeisk. You can't imagine it. But then, thank God, there were forest fires somewhere nearby. The smoke got rid of the mosquitoes. And the smoke filled our nostrils too. We had to work in the fields. That was the best of all the work we had to do, like tying up sheaves of corn. You could chew the grains. Sometimes my brigade had to look after pigs, there must have been several hundred. Nearby was a field of sunflowers, so we had more seeds to chew. At least our stomachs didn't rumble all the time. Every day we got thirty grams of sugar, gruel, cucumbers and carrots. Not bad at all.

Then we had to cut peat. First we had to cut it into a lot of pieces. We got very sunburnt, quite wrinkled, because we didn't have anything to oil our skin with. At last we got plank beds, in groups of four. You had to crawl in from the foot of the bed. But it didn't matter. Ruth, Frau Bandilla, the lady curate and I shared a big plank bed. Each of us had a mattress. It was filled with sawdust. Bed bugs crawled out of it. Sometimes our brigade leader threw us out in the night. Whenever she came back from a visit to her man. Delousing, scrubbing out the latrines, that sort of thing, in the middle of the night. Then you couldn't get the smell of the latrines out *of your nose. Or the smell of the delousing liquid. The lice bred in your armpits and in your pubic hair.*

Everything is so clean here in hospital. I can go to the toilet on my own as well. It is nearly always free when I want to go. In Kopeisk nearly all of us had diarrhoea all the time. We had enough charcoal tablets. One of the guards said we would soon be freed. No one would be there in the winter, we would go home. In Russian go home is damoy. *All the women talked about was what it was like at home.*

The following three lines have been thickly inked out. They are illegible even when they are held against the light. They were probably some sentences about feeling homesick, which she did not want anyone to read; the edge of the page has been decorated with sunflowers.

There is a ring at the garden gate. It is Interflora. Bea is not comforted by the fact that even from the clinic Jacob arranges for flowers to be sent to her, heavy, dense pink roses with buds between the thorns, and delphiniums. No sooner has one wilted bunch flown onto the compost heap than the next even prettier one arrives. Unfortunately the flowers merely serve to tell Bea that Jacob has a guilty conscience, because he shuts her out of his life. He didn't tell her which clinic he was going to. Really, how could he have sneaked off like that? In any case she had been amazed that he had fallen for *her*, of all people – a German, and one who looks the way she does. Bea thinks: 'It isn't true that I crossed his path in the right place and at the right time. Definitely not a stroke of luck. I didn't manage to cheer him up at all. Now he's making sure he can escape from our relationship relatively unscathed, sends a few more Jacob's flowers, as a gallant farewell. Jacob. Jacob. I'd really like to have named everything after him. But Jacob rose up and went on his way.'

Bea doesn't think he will contact her again, as he promised to do on the telephone. *When it's all over, I'll get in touch.* He wouldn't like her any more, anyway. She's put on two kilos. If she's not careful she'll get even fatter from all the worry. Is it really worth all these tears? What actually happened? She was permitted to show Doctor Stern the sights of Mark Brandenburg; she isn't permitted to sit next to his hospital bed. She was permitted to go out with him and invite him for meals; she wasn't permitted to set foot in his flat. She was permitted to try to cheer him up; she isn't permitted to share his fears. He kept her at a distance. She would have liked to send him letters in hospital. Bea does not know what Jacob's handwriting looks like. And he does not know hers. The more she thinks about it, the less likely it seems that they would be able to recognise themselves in the other's mental picture.

Should she have told Jacob about her mother? How would he have reacted to Frau Hiller's notes?

In Krüssen the women who were very ill were separated

from the others. They were allowed to go home. I'm sure none of them managed. Ruth wasn't ill enough any more, I wasn't either, yet. I only got diarrhoea when we were in Karabash. A lot of the women already had diarrhoea in Krüssen. They were given charcoal tablets. That was all. In Krüssen we slept in stables. And the food was disgusting, not even the pigs were fed food like that at home. Ruth said it made her stomach clench like a fist. That's just what it was like. But swallow it down. Hunger makes you shovel it in. They still counted us all the time. Whenever they took us to the cesspits. They were very deep, with thin boards on the top. Some people fell through.

On the way there and back we always passed other work brigades. Sometimes people recognised each other, even saw relatives. But they weren't allowed to talk to each other. Nothing. A guard would separate them straight away. My sister wasn't in any of the other work brigades. Ruth thought she might already have been sent back in Quakenburg, since she was only fifteen. They only took the ones who were over sixteen.

In Krüssen a woman saw her daughter. She wanted to go to her. She wouldn't let anyone hold her back. Nor would the daughter in the other brigade. So the shit of a guard knocked them both into the mud and kicked them with his boots. No one could do anything about it. They really hated us. I don't think that German soldiers did anything like that in Russia.

After ten or twelve days, we had to go on. Then we saw another terrible thing. What happened was that one woman went past her own home. She had left with the

other refugees in January. She couldn't bear it, she just
ran. First to the garden gate and then further. The
guards shouted 'stoy', but they started shooting almost at
once. The woman just lay there. When we went on,
Ruth said, 'My God, three steps from the front door,
I'd like it that way too.'

If only Bea had never found this text, which leaves
her lying awake at nights. Jacob would have been the
only person to whom she would gladly have given the
pages to read: 'This is what happened to my mother. I
think you should know.' She would also have had to
tell him that her mother had been searching for her
wounded father. But how does one say 'love'? How
does one begin to say it to someone whose parents
certainly died in an infinitely more degrading and
terrible way?

Jacob would probably have declined to read a
document written by a woman who was so devoted
to the Führer that, as she frankly writes, she would
have liked more than anything to change the first 'l' of
her surname, Hiller, into a 't'. When she said her
name, Frau Hiller always spoke a bit unclearly, to
make it sound like Hitler. She trusted the Führer's
words when they came out of the wireless, as though
they were gospel; and even in Konitz, when she heard
about Hitler's suicide, she said it was nonsense. And
when she finally wrote down what she remembered
in 1948, one of the last to be repatriated, Frau Hiller
would doodle at the side of each page on which

Hitler's name was written, a sort of crown of thorns made of little interlocking swastikas.

No, one could not expect Jacob to read all this. But why was Bea unable to tell it to him in her own words? In the end, who was hiding from whom? The burden of silence has been their undoing. They always talked about other things, other people, about Chekhov, about Fontane, about all sorts of things, as though to free themselves of everything they had learnt, read and known. Jacob could lecture her for hours on end about his extinct plants and the order in which they appeared in the history of the planet; about two-thousand-year-old magnolia seeds which had been found in the tombs of Egyptian pharaohs and had been made to germinate again today, even to blossom. He would describe the survival tactics of certain plants – lichens and mosses which live at the polar seas, for example, which only feel the warmth of the sun for two days a year and so develop plump cushions in which to store the little bit of heat. When Jacob's tongue was loosened by wine, he was filled with enthusiasm for botany's amazing, oddest phenomena, and she was only too pleased to listen.

But nothing he said had any relevance to himself. She found out next to nothing about him, and if she asked something he would look evasive, continuing to talk even more keenly about the plants, about their slow-motion lives and how one can reveal their infinitely patient development using time-lapse photography. He lectured, talked, went into detail. Bea asked questions and wanted to know things and sometimes thought to herself: 'Thank you so much for this conversation, Doctor Stern, but I would like to have asked different questions.'

Jacob had in her an attentive listener. He was always very grateful for that.

He had, he was. Does she already think of him in the past? 'Your laughter is contagious,' he once said. If her tears had been contagious as well, she would have been able to tell him how she is burdened by the discovery she made in the attic.

School begins again. The lessons tire Bea out more than ever. German. History. Religious instruction. She stands before her class; her pupils sit there like cartoon characters, each with a speech bubble coming out of its mouth, containing one of those clipped sentences they use when they speak, if they speak at all. Their quacking gets worse every year, particularly in religious instruction, the waffling subject which one can give up if one can't be bothered with it.

During her teacher training and in the years following it, Bea taught at a girls' school. That was really very pleasant. One did not need forty minutes to motivate the pupils before one could finally come to the point. Now the same girls – no, others, of course, in another school – loll around amongst the boys as though to say, 'So now, let's see how you're going to get through this lesson with us!' It is difficult to like them. They find nothing exciting any more. Nothing reaches them. Are they really as hard boiled as they appear? When they go up to the blackboard, they swing their hips as though the space between the desks were a catwalk and the boys a jury whose job it was to decide which of them has the most sex appeal. Using their whole bodies, they show the only thing that really matters to them, and the most intelligent ones seem to be able to do it best. Their ostentatious self-confidence worries Bea and annoys her. She gets on better with the boys; gruff as they are, she manages more easily to keep their attention from constantly straying. Though they all dress the same, she sees individual faces which she can tell apart. From time to time she even has favourites – that is, she must not let them see that she likes them especially but they sense it anyway, and she is pleased that even so they do not try to ingratiate themselves with her.

Still, all things considered, Bea lives from one weekend to the next, from one holiday to the next, and wonders how she can manage to take early retirement.

How many hospitals are there in Berlin? Bea could start telephoning them one after another and ask to be put through to Doctor Stern. Stern, yes, as in unyielding, first name Jacob as in the Bible, whose hip the angel put out of joint. But the patient was probably discharged long ago and is in the rehabilitation clinic, learning to walk again. Or he has retreated into his Lichterfelde refuge, a man who does not wish to be disturbed.

Bea has always travelled by public transport in town. Now she feels incapable of doing so, she becomes claustrophobic amongst so many people; the escalators advance relentlessly and the metal ridges under the steps throw her off; a cold wind blows out of the U-Bahn tunnels as though it were already December instead of September. Berlin is suddenly a Moloch-like Disney city full of booming noise and throngs of people and a hysteria of special offers; one cannot really see it any more.

Jacob's telephone number is not listed in the directory. Bea has respected his wish neither to be contacted by telephone nor visited. Now she remembers that he once mentioned the Soester Strasse, that it was still cobbled and that one could forget the big city there. She finds the Soester Strasse on the map, a short street in Lichterfelde West. And one day, towards evening, Bea drives there in her car and, looking very suspicious, goes from one garden gate to the next, from door to door, reading the nameplates. Stern?

Stern? Bea does not allow herself to listen to the ambiguity in the name. A dog barks intermittently. A young couple leaning against a garden gate extract themselves from their embrace.

'Are you looking for something?' asks the girl.

'I'm looking for a certain Doctor Stern.'

'That sounds like the Jew,' says the young man, and waves a hand, on the back of which a dragon is tattooed, towards a house set back a little from the road.

Bea goes to her car as though she wanted to fetch something from it, the young people's stares following her. When she returns, they have disappeared. The Soester Strasse lies deserted in the twilight, until all the street lamps light up at once and gradually the windows are illuminated; the only ones which remain dark are those of the low house which crouches among the spruce trees, no name on the garden gate. When Bea opens the gate, no dog starts to bark.

So, this is where Jacob hides himself, keeps people at bay and cares about nothing, as though one could just sweep aside the ways of the world. Since he stopped travelling, he has called up those bits of the world that he does want to see on his computer screen. As he has told Bea, he is a genius at the computer. Thanks to the multimedia, a click of the mouse brings *Rauwolfia* and his other poisonous plants variously magnified before his eyes; he can observe how an inconspicuous exotic plant paralyses its enemy by spraying poison. Jacob was a major contributor in a series of experiments in which the anti-hypertensive substance reserpine was successfully extracted from *Rauwolfia serpentina*, and since then he has been commissioned by an American group of companies to work on a publication about new methods being used in molecular biology to test plant substances for their possible medical effectiveness in future drugs.

Is his study on the garden side of the house? Is he sitting there, surrounded by a thousand books which turn their backs on him, is he hiding from her, smiling at the hopes she has snatched out of the Berlin air?

Bea now stands before a dark house she has never set foot in, and she ventures as far as the front door, which has no spy hole to distort her face beyond recognition. He who lives on hope dies of hunger, that was one of her grandmother's sayings. There is no nameplate on the front door either, but there is, as Bea can see in the light from her torch, a bell push. Jacob must have disconnected it, for however often Bea presses it the house stays deathly silent. And what would she have said if Jacob had opened the door? 'Hello! I'm the woman you met at the right place and the right time!'

Bea goes back to the pavement. What is she doing here? What business does she have in the Soester Strasse? Damn it, what business has she here? A man is coming towards her, talking to himself, but as he passes through the light of the street lamp Bea sees he is talking into a mobile phone. He passes by her, stops talking and walks more slowly. Bea suddenly finds herself thinking of the advice of her clever colleague: 'Whatever you do, don't cling! It will only end in tears. One can rent a man nowadays by the hour, go out with him, dance with him, sleep with him, and one can find the relationship quite satisfactory.' Unfortunately, in the Soester Strasse Bea fails to find comfort in irony.

A little dog comes along and sniffs at her shoes. Didn't Jacob tell her he had got himself a comical mongrel from the animal home in Lankwitz? This little dog, however, seems not to have an owner, it does not belong to a certain Doctor Stern. It walks past his house and further on along the fence. The man with the mobile phone comes back. He laughs loudly and says, 'That would be even nicer!' Then he pushes in the antenna and slips the phone into the breast pocket of his coat.

That time heals all wounds is not a very reliable truism. Pain and anger about Jacob's silence torment Bea. It is as though he has disappeared off the face of the earth. A ghost has been sending her flowers. Nevertheless, when she locks her garden gate in the evenings, she still looks down the road to see if her beloved is coming along. Then in November there are a great many shooting stars. But the time when wishing might have helped is past.

The first snow falls. The first night frost drives Bea out into the garden, as it does every year. The outside tap must be turned off, the pond drained, the hose unwound from its little cart and hung coiled up in the cellar – precautions that her grandfather used to be in charge of.

Working with her hands does her good. Bea spreads leaves on the flowerbeds and cuts back the hops by the fence. The long-stemmed roses are too old just to bend them down towards the soil, so she has to bind them at the top with spruce twigs. The sky looks as if it might snow again; she hopes it will be fine dry powder snow which lets the air in and keeps the earth warm. When snow falls in big flakes it quickly crusts over, it becomes heavy and is no use for anything.

In Karabash the snowflakes were three times as big as at home and three times as thick. Snow, snow. How would it all ever melt? In front of the hut window a wall of snow. Above, the fattest icicles. Thirty-five degrees below zero. Your blood really froze. Our teeth really chattered, we could hear them. They put thick logs on the floors of our huts, otherwise we would have frozen solid. We stuffed everything into the metal stove. Even bits of wood which we hacked off the walls. Two people went to the sick hut, two people died, so we burnt the whole big plank bed.

The guard in Karabash was called Boris. He always had one eye closed. He was mostly blind drunk anyway. His nose was bright red. And all gaps in his teeth. He looked very comical. But for a Russian he was nice, sometimes we could get a second helping of soup or kasha.

In Karabash there were also women who volunteered to be supervisors. They were called special-duty prisoners. Some of them were the Russians' whores. Everyone knew. But they still had to slave in the mine. We were taken there every morning. It wasn't far, maybe ten minutes. Everyone was given a hammer. It weighed twenty pounds, or even more. We got very thick leather spats and leather mittens, like gardening gloves but thicker. Still some people got blisters. We had to smash the hot iron up. That was after the first smelting. Then we had to load the pieces onto trucks. We did that non-stop. The truck came. We had to load it up. Then the next one came, and God help you if the other one wasn't full yet. Sometimes hot pieces fell down. It was murderous work. Death by instalments, said the lady curate, 'natural diminution of prisoners through work',

that's what we Germans showed people how to do, she
said, after all, with the Jews. But it was boiling hot in
there. And then the cold outside. You can't describe it.

At five o'clock work ended. By then it was pitch dark
already. The Soviet star hung over the camp gate. It was
completely covered with snow too. Every evening it lit up
from inside. There were light bulbs in it. Because of that
the snow kept melting. And it kept on snowing, like
mad. The snow turned red from the red light bulbs, and
melted. Ruth said, 'As if the star were weeping red
tears.' I won't forget that.

Frau Hiller seems to have had a good memory. She
even wrote down a verse of a song which the hated
brigade leader in Karabash often used to sing to the
others.

> *Moonlight gleamed on bayonets,*
> *On the sabre's hilt all white,*
> *We stood and sang and on our hats*
> *Red stars rose up in the night.*

Frau Hiller wrote pages about this brigade leader,
whose name was Hedwig. It seems she had to write it
all down, to free herself of it.

In Karabash it was Hell. But Hedwig purposely set out
to make it Hell for us. She was pregnant, but she
hadn't been there in Konitz. Some women were pregnant
from there. The ones who were still alive would have the

poor little mites soon. But Hedwig wasn't that far gone.
Who knows where it came from, it must have been from
a Russian.

In the evening we were dog-tired from the work. But
then Hedwig would give us lectures. They called it
'convincing'. We just had to listen. You couldn't block
your ears. Ruth said that Hedwig had discovered her
Bolshevik heart. Every evening she would start with the
song. God help whoever didn't sing along. They would
be made to suffer. We imitated her behind her back. She
particularly had it in for me, she was always shaking her
stick in my face. In Karabash we got padded jackets. To
me she gave a filthy one which didn't fit at all. And she
never gave me any earmuffs. Then she just ignored me,
and I was standing right at the front. But a lot of
women died in Karabash. They just didn't get up again
in the morning. So I got earmuffs too.

Boris said that all the women who were ill and the
ones who couldn't work any more would soon be allowed
to go. And then all the rest. No one believed it any
more. Boris also said that tiled stoves would soon be
installed in the huts. But that was just talk too. Three
women in my work brigade were pregnant from the rapes
in Konitz. In December two of them were still alive.
They were the only ones Hedwig had any sympathy for.
They were allowed to work in the sick hut.

Bea should hide Frau Hiller's diary back in the attic,
these belated revelations of her mother's fate. She
must not start it again, searching the map for the

stations of the cross: STOLP, SAGERITZ, QUA-
KENBURG, KRÜSSEN, BALDENBURG, RUM-
MELSBURG, KONITZ, SOLDAU, KORKINO,
KOPEISK, KARABASH. Otherwise she lives
through the whole thing in her imagination and it will
destroy her. She has already caught herself scratching
sometimes because her scalp is itching. But she *wasn't*
there, when her mother's hair was shorn. Whilst all
that was happening she was still in nappies, or was just
starting to walk.

For her Christmas holidays Bea should book herself a trip to a sunny island, far away from Berlin: all the way to New Zealand, where there is a lot of nature and very little world history. And she should fling the Interflora bouquets, the Jacob's flowers, onto the compost heap along with her fading hopes. There are so many flowers lying there that it will turn into the most fertile of fertilisers. If Bea tilled the soil with it, her garden would be perpetually in flower.

Bea has by now got to know the delivery man from the flower shop. He is always in a hurry and rings the bell twice, emphatically. She gives him five marks for each delivery.

The doorbell rings twice, emphatically. Why are today's flowers arriving in the evening? With a five-mark piece in her hand, she stands at the front door. The face in the distorting mirror looks like Munch's *The Scream*. Bea's heart misses a beat.

Jacob! Good God, she must give him back his nice face. Un-made up as she is, her hair unwashed, she opens the door and does what she should have done long ago, flinging her arms round his neck so wildly that he loses his stick, and kissing the flimsy apologies from his lips: no, he shouldn't say anything, he isn't disturbing her, he isn't just popping in, he isn't leaving in a minute, he's staying with her.

She would like to prepare a meal in the kitchen but the fridge is empty, she's on one of her diets again. But there are potatoes and apples, so Bea's hands fly to conjure up her grandmother's recipe, 'Heaven and Earth'.

He has brought his wine with him, a Rheingau-Riesling, *Beerenauslese*. Do they need Dutch courage? Do they leave the table after dinner a bit tipsy? Jacob does not want to sit on the sofa behind the dining table, he wants to go into the dark bedroom. Bea takes his glasses off and lays them on the bedside table. Rather clumsily, he pulls the pins from her hair. They do not need to tear their clothes off. They have the whole night long to become lovers, and when they awake the next morning, they have surely been dreaming the same dream. They must be the happiest couple in Berlin.

Bea's bedroom is her refuge. When she goes to bed at night she likes to be able to imagine that her grandparents are singing her the song about the fourteen angels which surround her, and she likes to be able to wake up feeling as though the new day will bring what the previous one still owes her, and which could perfectly well happen if reality were not so boring and miserable.

She has only recently finished furnishing her

bedroom. Curtains, rugs and bedspread in her favourite colours, blue and green. The most exquisite furniture: pale Finnish birch, the large wardrobe with eight mirrored doors and adjustable shelves. But on the wall of the large bedroom, on the one which is reflected in the mirrors, the one on which the morning light and Bea's waking glance fall, hangs the inherited ancestral picture gallery: *The Flight into Egypt*, a Reich's print after Dürer's woodcut; next to it Millet's *Angelus* and a framed photograph of Rodin's *The Kiss*; the portrait of a set of great-grandparents, whom she did not know; and the wedding photograph of her parents, whom she also did not know, her father in the uniform of a lance-corporal of the Wehrmacht, her mother wearing a dream of white chiffon, a myrtle wreath in her hair; underneath hang a child's drawings and a yellow crescent moon with a cord dangling from it, and a jumping jack with a string hanging down too: if you pull it, he draws up his arms and legs. And there are other things hanging on the wall too, things which have had their day and are of no concern to anyone.

Bea would never have allowed Jacob into her bedroom without having first removed a few items from the wall. She fears his sarcasm. But there he is, lying in her bed, and in the morning the pitiless light falls on *The Flight into Egypt* and on the lance-corporal of the Wehrmacht, on the yellow crescent moon and on the other bits and pieces, all reflected in the mirrors, sentimental, corny things which used to move the little girl to tears.

Bea quickly gets out of bed to go into the bathroom and then prepare a decent breakfast. Does Jacob drink tea or coffee in the morning? Does he like his egg hard or soft boiled, in a glass or scrambled? Would he like muesli, toast, wholemeal bread? She bustles about in the kitchen and does not know whether Jacob is meanwhile inspecting the perfidious picture gallery in the bedroom, shaking his head, or if he is pulling the string under the crescent moon, which sets the musical box tinkling Brahms' lullaby. Maybe Jacob will think what he has already observed on other occasions, that she always has to push so much feeling to one side before she can get to the point.

When they are facing each other at the breakfast table, he makes no reference at all to her bedroom and its four walls. Nevertheless, she feels as transparent as a child caught doing something it shouldn't, and she is annoyed because she wants to disown her father and her mother and the little girl at the abyss, and the angel.

Jacob asks about the pretty china she has used to make the table look so beautiful: 'Meissen? Or Nymphenburg?'

'Berlin, Royal Factory.'

'Immortal. It'll last for ever. One shouldn't buy china like this, one must inherit it. You inherited it, didn't you?'

'From my grandparents, yes, on my mother's side.

The Chippendale furniture came from them too. I want to leave everything the way it always was in this room, perhaps because I'm the last one left.'

She would like to tell Jacob now about her grandparents and her childhood in this house. He would certainly listen politely, but then he would probably dismiss the subject with an ironic remark, pointing out, for instance, that despite her upbringing she has become a perfectly acceptable person. He has said that once already. If she could tell him about her find in the attic, and what happened to her mother, he would doubtless react differently. But how? Would she try to dismiss it, perhaps remarking that, after all, the Germans did start the war? He knows that Bea's parents died in 1945. When she mentioned it once, he said that then they were both leftovers, two of a kind. About himself and his own family, he has not yet said a word. Bea must be the one to break the silence between them. But before she can find the right words, Jacob leaves the table, murmuring an apology, goes into Bea's study and returns after a bit holding a book. 'Joseph Brodsky,' he says. '*Less Than One*. I noticed you had it.'

Flicking through the book, he quickly finds the page where Brodsky describes the parquet floor of his parents' 'room and a half' in Leningrad, how he was never allowed to walk around in socks because his mother strongly objected to such sloppy habits and in any case was afraid that he might slip on the polished wood. When her son later lived in exile in America, he could have gone around on the Canadian maple floorboards barefoot even, to his heart's content, but he did not, because his mother would not have approved of it. He wanted to keep things the way they were in his family, now that he was the only one left.

This morning Bea once again fails to turn the conversation around to her mother. What she wants to say remains unsaid. Jacob walks round and round the table, still holding Brodsky's *Less Than One*, and starts talking about the Christmas holidays. What would she think of their travelling somewhere together? And what about to St Petersburg?

Jacob wants to go to the Hermitage, he wants to see Rembrandt's magnificent *Danaë* and his *Return of the Prodigal Son*, Leonardo's *Benois Madonna* and Raphael's *Madonna and Child*. He wants to see Caspar David Friedrich's *Moon Rising Over the Sea* and Max Liebermann's *Girl in the Field*, and last but not least the prehistoric finds from the frost-graves of the Altai Mountains: it would be interesting for him in view of new research into extinct plants. Bea can really have no idea how long St Petersburg has been at the top of the list of places he'd like to visit – even when it was still called Leningrad it was his dream destination, only the damned political situation prevented him from going. There are even some of the art treasures looted in the war on display now, long-lost masterpieces from private German art collections, including one

Renoir which he absolutely has to show her, for it is painted music.

Jacob's art of persuasion is inspiring, she knows that by now; he baits his line to tempt her to come with him to St Petersburg in the middle of the freezing winter. He has already found out everything, down to the last detail: one can get there without any problem at all, a non-stop flight by Lufthansa, or else by Scandinavian Airlines, change in Copenhagen; or by Finnair, change in Helsinki; or, if one wants, by boat from Bremerhaven, on the *Maxim Gorki*, stopping off in Danzig (now Gdansk), Königsberg (now Baltysk, or is it now Kaliningrad or Kantgrad?), change in Riga (still Riga), in Reval (now Tallinn), and back via Helsinki and Stockholm. Of course, on a cruise like that one's time is restricted, there would only be two days left for St Petersburg, not nearly enough to see the art treasures and the prehistoric finds from the frost-graves. At the travel agent's he asked for some brochures: from England you could travel on the *Silver Cloud*, on what they call an adventure holiday, but you still couldn't stay in any city longer than two days, and anyway the atmosphere on board a luxury liner like that would be unbearable: there was a disco, a bistro, fitness studios with a whirlpool and an aerobics room with a sprung floor. Good God, the whole fitness clique would be gathered on that old tub, maybe real joggers could even go running over the water, and in the evenings they'd all link arms and sway from side to side and a band would play songs and they'd all sing along, Jacob shuddered at the thought – no, one must, they really must fly instead, in a few hours they would be there.

Amazing that Jacob has not already booked the flight, for two passengers, naturally, for him and for her.

Bea can have absolutely no idea for how long he has wanted to go to St Petersburg, only first a huge empire had to crumble and the Berlin Wall fall down before he could achieve his heart's desire. 'Would you like to come too?' Jacob does not really expect an answer to his question. He takes it for granted that Bea will be happy to be taken along. And yes, she is happy. But does it really have to be Russia, of all places? Does it have to be St Petersburg? And at this time of year?

Thirty-five degrees below zero. Your blood really froze. Our teeth really chattered.

She can already hear her teeth chattering. But she will go. What else can she do? She is being permitted to accompany him to his dream destination, she's the woman on whom he's bestowing his favour. She knows how much he used to enjoy travelling. He always wanted to be anywhere other than where he was. Nowhere was he at home. He will not feel at home at her house in Grunewald, either. She will be his travelling companion and his lover. What more can she want?

Now he makes the trip to Russia sound alluring.

72

Now he tempts her with St Petersburg. There are numerous ways to get there, all roads lead to St Petersburg, so to speak, by sea, by land, by air. By land, by air? What would happen if Bea were to suggest to Jacob that they travel by ship, despite the disco and the fitness studio, that they drive to Bremerhaven in her car, making a detour through Pomerania, through the former Hinterpommern, that is, via Stolp (now Slupsk), via Sageritz (which, as Bea has learnt, was renamed Zagorsyca). Jacob can really have no idea how long she has wanted to go to Stolp and Sageritz. And on her map Stolp and St Petersburg are very close together. Bea wants to go to Stolp. It is not only the political situation which has kept her from going till now. But what on earth, Jacob would ask her, would you want to go to Stolp for, to Sageritz? What on earth for? For heaven's sake, I'll tell him, in Stolp, in Sageritz . . . but he would ask where is it anyway, is it in the former Hinterpommern? Would it not be completely misguided to drive through Hinterpommern, and on icy roads as well?

The roads were completely iced over. The ice didn't even crack underfoot. Every day thirty to thirty-five kilometres. Sometimes it was through the woods. At least the wind wasn't so bad there. Even the mist was frozen between the trees. But we still had our own warm things on then. Once two girls tried to run away. When we were allowed to stop for a bit, they ran off into the woods. The Russians didn't notice at first. But then they did

*when they counted us again. Two are missing. The girls
must have got quite far because the shots came from far
away.*

Even if Jacob did not ask her what on earth she
wanted to go to Hinterpommern for, the word Stolp
would make him pause. Stolp? Stolp? Didn't Gottfried
Benn work there as a captain in the medical corps
during the war? Jacob's voice would take on its
relentless tone. Once he actually starts talking about
the era of National Socialism, his lungs cannot give
him enough breath for all the words and names.

'Gottfried Benn?' he said, when he found Benn's
collected works on Bea's bookshelves. 'Gottfried
Benn? In 1933 he sang the praises of the New Youth
who were rallying under Hitler's star. And the views
that he, the poet, held about the desirability of a slave
state and about "selective breeding" were as solemn as
they were half baked, and less pretentiously formu-
lated they spelt Auschwitz. It makes absolutely no
difference that the poet rather quickly turned into a
radical sceptic.'

Jacob knows no mercy. Bea is sure he could quote
word for word the vision Benn had at that time. But
Jacob's spiteful tone annoys her. There is nothing
cheaper than mocking someone's misjudgement with
hindsight. That Benn was banned from writing and
completely revised his ideas counts for nothing with
Jacob. Bea does not feel able to confess that she
includes a considerable number of Benn's poems in

74

her poetry repertoire. Though in her German classes she can no longer expect her pupils to read poetry, and certainly not expressionist poetry.

As one might have predicted, they are not going to sail on a luxury liner from Bremen, they are going to fly non-stop to St Petersburg. But at least Bea has succeeded in making Jacob understand that she is not willing to sacrifice the whole of her holidays to this winter trip to Russia. He has therefore booked two single rooms at the Hotel Moskva just from 22 to 29 December. 'That would be agreeable to you, wouldn't it?'

Ever since she has known Jacob she has found it difficult to say what is and what is not agreeable to her. Most of the time she feels that she is compliant to the point of submissiveness, as though she has exchanged her own life for a new one ready made for her by Jacob, as though she would do everything that she does not really want to do. She is afraid of flying. If necessary, she would have flown to the warm south at this time of year, but she is going to travel three thousand kilometres north. She likes it best when she is at home for Christmas, and yet she declares her readiness to leave on 22 December. Jacob decides things, as though they were an old married couple for whom it goes without saying that the man plays the dominant role.

'That would be agreeable to you, wouldn't it?' is another of those questions, the sort that does not expect an answer; and his warning that she should pack warm clothes sounds threatening rather than solicitous: 'Pack warm things so that you won't need to moan about the cold. After all, I can't keep you warm the whole time.' No, he didn't say that about keeping her warm. Bea hears a lot of things too which she would like to hear.

She finds all her warmest clothes and buys a pair of expensive fur-lined boots at Bally. Had it been a different time of year, and had they not been travelling to Russia, she would certainly not have had to think of her mother while she was packing, of the imitation leather suitcase and the green rucksack. Grandfather took his daughter to the railway station. Bea forgot to ask him how they managed to get through Berlin during the blackout and at the crack of dawn, and from which station trains left for the north at the end of February 1945. Had there still been reliable timetables of any sort?

The plane takes off from Tegel Airport for St Petersburg at nine forty-five. Jacob lets Bea have the window seat. He reaches past her to press the button on her right arm rest, to put her seat upright. He carefully checks that her seat belt is fastened. Does he have a bad conscience because he persuaded her to accompany him to Russia in the middle of winter?

Once the captain's voice has greeted the passengers in English, Russian and German, it requests them to keep their seat belts fastened as there may be turbulence. A red-haired flight attendant tells them where the emergency exits are located and how to open them should the occasion arise, accompanying her instructions with a sort of sign language. Bea looks out of the window. The sharp angle which the wing makes with the ground opens up like a fan. The resurrected city is revealed as they climb, ever neater and more clearly defined: the old museum and the cathedral on the Spreeinsel, the leafless black Lustgarten and the Marx-Engels-Platz, which is now called the Schlossplatz again, and behind wire netting the former Platz der Republik. From this bird's eye view a round and an oval lake look as if they are frozen over, and they probably are: the thermometer on Bea's balcony showed minus fourteen degrees earlier this morning. Before leaving the house, she put Frau Hiller's notes into her shoulder bag; maybe there will be an opportunity after all to show them to Jacob or to read them to him.

A jet plane flies at nine hundred kilometres an hour, so they could soon be flying over Hinterpommern, over Stolp, over Sageritz, over Slupsk, over Zagorsyca. *The place was called SAGERITZ.* The name in block capitals, underlined. *So the lady curate brought the poor woman back to Sageritz in her cart.* Bea thinks: SAGERITZ, my 'So that's where they went from'.

While they sip their hot tea, she strictly forbids herself to think about her mother. Tonight Jacob will come to her room and take the pins from her hair. Her hair is the only bit of her worth seeing: honey blond, Jacob says it is, and like leaves. He likes to cover his face with it or wind it around his wrist. Since Bea has known him she has made her hair almost into a cult, brushing her golden locks like the Lorelei, falling for every advertisement that promises more volume, more shine. *Energy right to the tips.* She plucks out every grey strand, though one would not really notice them in her blond hair.

Her mother must have had even more beautiful, thick hair. But how could Bea tell Jacob that they had cut off her plait and shaved her head? He would probably reply that they had certainly cut off his mother's hair too (dark brown, contrary hair, like his own?) and that they had made felt slippers out of bleached, spun Jews' hair. Jacob's mother, Bea's mother. The future generations are united by a sort of conflicting common ground: they prefer to say nothing. *A wide rift of silence* lies between them, *a high wall of night* – *mon dieu*, Benn again, a name Bea can't even utter any more.

Jacob is looking through a guide book to St Petersburg. Bea wants to nestle her hands in his. Her hands are much more eloquent than her lips. Hands don't feel the need to admit that one knows very little about the other person and is asking even less: afraid of interfering in someone else's life, careful not to go too far – for all sorts of reasons one would rather say too little than too much, a silent agreement which seems appropriate to their relationship. From time to time, Bea has the feeling that Jacob would like to tell her something, but without making himself vulnerable in the process.

As they approach St Petersburg she would like to rest her head against his shoulder. But she sits as one is supposed to sit, quiet and numbed in her upright seat. Already over the looking-glass surface of Lake Peipus, the nose of the plane starts to dip. But it is still a long time until the panorama of the city in winter appears on the horizon, a picture-postcard skyline behind a curtain of snow, a scene that Bea's father, as part of

the advance guard, saw through his binocular periscope. St Petersburg, still called Leningrad at that
time, of course, was besieged and starved for eight
hundred and eighty days. According to Hitler's vision,
the city was to be wiped off the map.

If Bea cannot tell Jacob about her father here, then
where will she ever be able to? How will he take it?
Will he listen to her or will he interrupt and shame
her: 'Your father was at the siege of Leningrad? I
don't believe it!' Will he enumerate for her what no
one need enumerate for her: the countless numbers of
people who starved and froze to death in the
blockade, during which the city was without water,
electricity, heating, without a sewage system, without
any means of burying the dead. Jacob would consider
the Berlin blockade, on the other hand, a compara-
tively trivial episode, although the Berliners suffered
quite badly. In the winter of 1943–44, the people of
Leningrad ate boiled shoe leather, minced dogs and
cats, rats and mice, and cannibalism was an everyday
occurrence.

Did Bea's father have any idea of the extent of the
misery? Through his binocular periscope could he
make out the mountain of frozen bodies on the
outskirts of the city, the sledges carrying the corpses
away, the snowdrifts which reached the first floor of
those houses which were still standing? From one of
his letters it is clear that he did have some idea of the
way things were in the city he was fighting. He writes
to his wife: 'If only you could help me feel shame.'

Even so, Bea would not be brave enough to let Jacob read her father's letters.

Bea sees the aileron flap up. Jacob leans towards her and asks her something she does not understand. She shrugs her shoulders, lifts her hands with splayed fingers to her blocked ears and shouts, 'What did you say?' He opens his mouth so wide that she can see past the gold fillings in his teeth to his uvula, and then she remembers that one is supposed to yawn to unblock one's ears. So she yawns as widely as she can, as though she were awakening from a long sleep. When at last the plane lands, bumpily, she cuddles up for a moment against Jacob: it doesn't matter if he knows how much she likes sheltering in his arms. After all, quite often she has the feeling that he needs her just as much as she needs him.

On their arrival at the Hotel Moskva it becomes apparent that the two single rooms they booked are unavailable, *leider Gottes*, laments the head porter at reception, in fluent German, alas! they are having problems with water damage, with burst pipes. He is inconsolable and apologises for the inconvenience; there are problems with the central heating as well. Neither a generous tip nor exaggerated politeness are of any help to the couple in obtaining two single rooms.

'And now what are we supposed to do?' Jacob is beginning to lose his composure, as if the Great Flood had begun.

'My dear sir, we will find a solution!'

After a lot of toing and froing, while Jacob curses under his breath – Russian economy . . . bloody mess . . . icebox – the solution is in the end one double bedroom. Bea is secretly amused, gives some money to the woman who accompanies them through the long corridors, and finds out that one wing of the enormous hotel has been temporarily closed since there are so few tourists at this time of year, to save energy at night.

The double room is warm, large and cosy, and it has a very wide double bed with a fringed bedspread and one cushion lying on it. One door leads to the bathroom, another into a loggia. To cheer Jacob up, Bea suggests sawing the double bed in two and putting one half in the loggia, which is not heated of course, but they could toss a coin to decide who should sleep in the warm and who in the cold. Jacob gives her a quick kiss and asks what they will do if he snores too horribly.

'You don't snore. That's one thing I've discovered by now.'

'Well, I'm not so sure.'

'All right, sometimes you do snore a bit. I once read that you should whistle, then the other person stops snoring.'

'You're amazing,' says Jacob, and sits down on one of the two wicker chairs. 'You won't even admit that I snore, let alone the fact that I'm quite incapable of living with someone else in a confined space.'

'It's fine if you want to smoke, it doesn't bother me a bit.'

'As I say, you're amazing.'

Relieved, Jacob fills his pipe. He rummages around laboriously for his lighter. Bea stops herself telling him that he always puts it in the left breast pocket of his jacket; he should not feel she is mothering him.

A lone wolf like this was unprepared for a double room with a double bed. Bea on the other hand is working out how much cheaper their stay at the hotel will be now.

'Did you say something?'

'No, not really.'

In precarious situations she is always impressed by her clever hands. She organises the room, making it into their love nest for the coming week. She moves the second wicker chair and the little wicker table nearer to the radiator, places the standard lamp next to them, and carries the fringed bedspread and the stiff cushion into the loggia. Out here, frost flowers have blossomed out of ice crystals on the lofty window panes, radiant, rampant. Bea has not seen patterns like this since her holidays in the Harz Mountains: ferns, needles, finely branching panicles, umbels, prisms, each piercing the next. Bea tries in vain to breathe a hole in the whiteness; she becomes dizzy but her breath is not hot enough: the spot on which she is breathing freezes over again before she can even catch a glimpse of what is outside.

Then she starts unpacking her suitcase. As she puts her underwear and jumper tidily into the wardrobe, she knows that Jacob has assumed his amused smile. Without turning round to look at him, she warns him not to call her Gretchen, or a 'German Gretchen', because he sometimes does that when he comes into her tidy house or neat garden.

'Don't you dare say it.'

'I haven't said a word!'

Bea knows how he sees her: efficient, orderly, punctual, reliable, blue-eyed, cheery and, on top of everything else, religious, all of which makes her for him a 'German Gretchen'. A woman with such substantial qualities does not cause trouble. His picture of her is complete, as though she were a pop-up person. This, along with the idea that he assumes she leads a smug and luxurious life in her beautiful home, all this infuriates her. But if Bea really were to become furious, Doctor Stern would stare at her as if she were a phenomenon, a little plant he had never come across before in his botanical gardens. Now, what have we here? Can't he see that Bea's so-called virtues are simply attempts to endure the absurdity of this hunchbacked existence? For a few weeks after reading Frau Hiller's notes, she set new records in sports as though she were in training for world championships; to try to get over the shock, she went cycling for hours on end, swam furious lengths, put on African music at home and danced until she dropped, as though to prove to herself that she was still alive, or to dance herself into a trance where she could achieve an ecstatic reunion with her mother.

If Jacob could have seen her . . . it doesn't bear thinking about.

★

The telephone rings. It is the head porter, personally enquiring if everything in their room is satisfactory. If sir and madam wish, he could arrange for hot water bottles to be put in their bed.

They would be glad if he did – though in any case they are going to warm each other up. If Jacob would just start unpacking his suitcase, they could go to the restaurant. Bea is starving. Or does he expect her to unpack his suitcase as well? Better to swallow down her 'Oh–come–on–then–let–me–do–it'. She walks round the double bed and opens the drawer of the bedside table. Inside is a brochure: 'Russian for Beginners, German–Russian, Russian–German'. *We must learn Russian, that's the most important thing now.* Bea's mother hardly had time to learn Russian. She did not survive the first Siberian winter.

Most of us were destroyed by the cold in Karabash. The sick hut was full. Frostbite, burns, typhus. More and more sick women were crammed in. Always two people to a bed. Every day a few of them died. That made room for the next ones. The lady curate couldn't keep up with her prayers for the dying. She said she'd had two thousand souls in Sageritz, the people had died of old age and she'd had at most one burial a month. Well, nothing would make me want to be a curate.

She was always allowed into the hospital hut. Day and night. When Ruth was brought in, she sometimes took me with her in secret. So I could visit Ruth. I would always toast some bread on the oven. I'd break it

into little pieces and feed it to her. Sometimes I mixed
in some potatoes boiled in their skins, and some borsch.
Real pig-swill. But Ruth was pleased to have something
to eat. The borsch made your urine red. Then you
didn't know what was blood and what was red colour.
Ruth wasn't well at all. A shadow of herself, as they
say. But she was still ashamed. Only at the very end,
she didn't care any more. I think she envied each person
that was taken out. The earth was frozen like stone. So
they just laid the bodies behind the walls of snow. One
on top of the other.

They left no traces behind in the snow. No moulds of
their bodies, like those on the Grunewald station wall,
the Wailing Wall, which makes Jacob shudder when
he sees it. Bea thinks: 'He has to pass it every time he
comes to see me.'

But in St Petersburg she cannot tell Jacob about the
winter in Karabash, nor about the sick hut where life
and death were laid bare, nor about quite other frost-
graves than the prehistoric ones in the Altai Mountains. Where should she put Frau Hiller's document?
She slips it beneath a pile of underwear in the
wardrobe, along with her little New Testament and
the Psalms, but Jacob tells her from the window, and
the wicker chair creaks, that she should feel free to
open her Psalms; after all everyone has to find their
own salvation. And how would Jacob condescend to
find his own salvation, in the name of God and
Jehovah? Bea knows what he would say if he had to

reply to such earnest questions: that, unfortunately, these assurances purporting to the deeper meaning of life make no sense to him. He does not understand them. He does not even want to start thinking about them. But she should feel free to read her Psalms if it makes her happy – or would he say, if it comforts you? Her Psalms. As though they were not much more *his*, since people were already reciting them in Israel when the Teutons were still hunting bears, as Bea's grandfather used to say. But Jacob would rather bite his tongue off than talk about 'his Psalms'. He says 'your' to Bea as he would say 'your business'. Education being more important to him than any-thing else, he has of course taken note of what is written there, no doubt about it, otherwise he would not recognise Bea's quotations from the Bible. He is no aesthete, he would not read the Psalms simply for his own edification or as an interesting vision of Utopia: *Rebuke those wild beasts of the reeds, that herd of bulls, the bull-calf warriors of the nations, who bring bars of silver and prostrate themselves. Scatter these nations which delight in war . . . The boots of earth-shaking armies on the march, the soldiers' cloaks rolled in blood, all are destined to be burned, food for the fire.* Even Bea's pupils sit up and listen to that. In a rare good lesson, she can discuss this sort of explosive material with them. But not with Jacob. She always thinks she knows how he will answer: 'If God let his chosen people – whom he had promised to cherish like life itself – go into the fire, I don't really need to read the story about the three men in the fiery furnace and the Psalms. Do I?'

Bea thinks that Jacob would be able to counter with twisted quotations from the Bible: *As sorrowful, and not rejoicing . . . The scattered and not united . . .* Oh for heaven's sake, why does she keep putting words into Jacob's mouth which he has never uttered?

In the bathroom, Bea arranges her toilet articles in one half of the cabinet over the basin. Only the cosmetics she needs for her hair stay in her sponge bag. Jacob doesn't have to see them. She should really put her watch two hours forward, but she leaves it as it is: she would not be able to stop herself thinking about Krüssen, 1945, and the shrieking farmer's wife from Masuren whose face Bea's mother slapped when she saw the hands of the watch being put forward, and panicked. Will Bea have to live with such images for the rest of her life, hear her mother's voice: *Don't drive us all mad as well!*

The mirror shows her her mother's heart-shaped hairline. Her grandmother used to tell her, *You're the spitting image of your mother.* She moves the wings of the mirror so that she can see her profile, right and left, sees her lips move as though she were standing in the wings and prompting the leading lady in a play entitled *The Abduction* or just *My Mother*. But it was not a play. It cannot be reconstructed, even though she knows by heart whole sentences which Frau Hiller wrote down, like: *Then Ruth said, I had a dream that I was going home, but even in the dream I knew that it was just a dream.*

Pochemu? Why? What's going on? The voice is Jacob's voice. Bea goes back into the bedroom, still holding her sponge bag. But she is mistaken. Jacob did not say anything: he has nodded off in the wicker chair. Even through the lids one can see the darkness of his eyes, eyes that never laugh when his mouth laughs. No, no, he is not dreaming, as his namesake did, of the ladder, the top of it reaching to heaven, and the angels of God ascending and descending on it. His fear of what has not yet happened but could happen again is written on his face. Bea caresses his face without touching it, her gaze kissing the blue veins which stand out endearingly on his temples, the deep lines running from nose to mouth, which one could not in Jacob's case call laughter lines. His mouth is thankfully free of moustache or beard. The lips are slightly parted, already chapped by the Siberian cold. One can hear his light breathing; he is not asleep, just slumbering. His face is expressionless. On his chin is a little stubble, silver grey. Unshaven like this, he looks twice as defenceless. For one endless moment he looks as though he has been entrusted to her. She thinks: 'If my mother had met a Jacob in her time, she would have been contravening paragraph 2.5, section 2 of the Nuremberg Laws, prohibiting sexual relations with non-Aryans.'

Slowly she zips up her sponge bag. She can feel her heart pulsing in her fingertips. She wants to lay Jacob's right hand, which is hanging down, on his knee and take off his glasses, but her touch would wake him. She looks at him and thinks that they would have killed him too, if they had caught him. Time and again, the past comes shuffling up in its grey felt slippers, made from women's hair, bleached and then spun.

Why has Jacob never told her how he managed to escape as a child? What is he barricading himself behind? From Doctor Kurz, Bea has only found out that Jacob's mother was able to leave the seven-year-old boy in a market garden and nursery in Berlin because the gardener, a woman, was under some sort of obligation to her. Kurz said that if his friend had not spent two years living in a hothouse, he would definitely not have become a botanist.

A child, hidden in a hothouse with clear glass windows. Bea sees it like a television image with the volume turned down. Who hid the boy? Who looked after him? How could it have been possible for a seven-year-old not to give himself away? Not to make a sound, not to cry, not to scream? Will Jacob ever find a way out of his inveterate silence? A swarm of question marks.

In Greater Germany during the time of National Socialism, his fate was sealed at the moment of his birth. The mere fact that he had been born meant that he and others like him were declared vermin. That was what made it impossible to compare them with the other victims. A past that does not pass. And he would have been barbarically persecuted here too, in the fifties, in St Petersburg (that is, Leningrad); he would have been reviled as a 'rootless cosmopolitan' and, had Comrade Stalin not died just in time, he would have been deported to Siberia. Perhaps to

Korkino. To Kopeisk. To Karabash. The camps were there, fully equipped, for the Soviet Final Solution, camps where torture, manslaughter and murder were everyday events. Stalin's secret service chiefs tracked down anyone who did not follow the one correct way of thinking; just having a Jewish-sounding name sufficed to put someone under suspicion.

If Jacob opened his eyes now, he would see Bea standing there and looking at him and he would know once and for all that she really did cross his path at the right moment. And she knows that without the beginning of his story he is not to be had. She tiptoes to the bed and lies down. The bed doesn't creak. She does not need to fetch her Psalms from the wardrobe, they are already in her head, words which are strong enough for the darkness: *Save me, O God; for the waters are come in unto my soul. I am weary of crying: my throat is dried.*

Next day, they go to the Hermitage. The Russian taxi driver tells them in heavily accented German how they can pass from one room to the next without getting lost; he often used to visit the art collection, art used to belong to the people, but now the tickets are expensive and he can't afford to look at the pictures any more. He doesn't know whether the museums are closed on Christmas Day, he has never celebrated Christmas: taking days off like that would ruin his business.

The prehistoric finds from the frost-graves of the Altai Mountains, which are the reason Jacob wanted to come to St Petersburg, can only be visited on the following day, if a visitor particularly wants to see them. 'Frost-graves' is still a phrase which for Bea belongs to Karabash.

In the Hermitage, they go first of all to look at the paintings of the Dutch School. Bea is so amazed by the precious floors and coffered ceilings that, gazing upwards, she stumbles and loses her balance, but she regains control and, while Jacob watches, executes a pirouette, expertly bending her knees and then up on the tips of her toes. Jacob once again shakes his head, and says he envies her her wonderful joints; he wouldn't be surprised if she could belly-dance.

Standing before Jan Gossaert's *Descent from the Cross*, Jacob points out how a soldier is setting the crown of thorns to one side: 'Look how carefully he's holding it. To my knowledge, that isn't depicted in any other painting of this biblical scene.' At Rembrandt's *Return of the Prodigal Son*, Jacob admires how all the light is concentrated on the shaven head of the son and on the face and hands of the father: 'Because of the brilliant use of light, the alert observer perceives the recovery behind the loss, the "Eat, drink and be merry!" The scene gains even more dramatic impact from the incomparable use of chiaroscuro in the background.'

They go from one painting to the next, and they hold hands. The double bedroom they were compelled to take has not proved in the least inimical to love. Here in St Petersburg they are lovers who deserve to be so called. This morning when Jacob awoke and, rubbing the sleep from his eyes, saw Bea, his eyes laughed too. As she came out of the bathroom he was sitting on the edge of the bed, his bare feet were fishing for his slippers and his pyjama trousers had slipped down under his stomach. Laughing, he said, 'Am I dreaming?'

In the German collection, Jacob pulls her over to Liebermann's *Girl in the Field*. 'Look at this. Did you by any chance sit for this painter?' He shows her the girl's profile and Bea sees herself sitting on the grass, looking at the two goats which are grazing behind the big vicarage in the valley. The sudden juxtaposition of these images brings back the taste of the goat's milk which she had to drink warm from the udder; her aunt said one did not need to boil it since goats do not carry tuberculosis. There was a pig in the yard, called Wanda, which sniffed out truffles under the humus in the oakwoods. There was a hothouse where flowers were grown all year round, carnations, freesias, gladiolae, stock, chrysanthemums. Bea's aunt sold the flowers and the truffles for a little extra income, and used the money for singing lessons. She sang in the church. Her voice seemed quite separate from the rest of her: no one would have suspected this slender, flat-chested woman of having such a powerful voice. Purely and effortlessly she hit the high notes. She used to stand in the organ loft. The congregation had their backs turned to her but Bea could see her from her seat in a side pew, could see how her shoulders rose and fell and how her arms fluffed up like folded wings, and then the singer would be standing there again, frozen, as if she had been listening to herself. She never read from the music when she sang. Now Bea sees that her singing was a way of releasing her repressed screams: her only son had died in the last weeks of the war. Her voice sang: *Christenleiden hat sein Mass und muss endlich stille stehn,* and *Wenn der Winter ausgeschneiet . . .*

When Bea was small, the small village church was big. The futile attempt to sit still, as if her hands had nothing better to do than to be folded, her feet to dangle, her mouth to keep silent. From above, carved up by the ribs of the mullioned windows, the much-praised morning light shone in, slowly shifting round during the sermon. The organ was decrepit, hic-coughing each time it drew breath. When the congregation was finally allowed to sing, Bea would have liked to sing on and on, more and more verses: no hymn was long enough for her. One of the two angels which floated above the pulpit sang with its mouth opened wide, the other, bigger, blew the trumpet in accompaniment, his cheeks puffed to bursting; and the exhausted figure killed on the Cross bowed his head. Right at the top, the triangular eye of God watched from the keystone.

How the sexton knew exactly when to pull the bell rope to anticipate the congregation's Amen, he never revealed to anyone; only that in the belltower, bells swinging back and forth, the bats could find their way in the dark, past all the ropes and traps, past the spiders' webs – that he did tell Bea, and he wanted to take her up into the tower to show her the bats which he said hung there upside-down. But she never went with him because she was afraid of him and because anyway she did not believe all that about the bats. The sexton wasn't quite right in the head, Bea's aunt used to say, he had been buried alive in the war, but there was no need to be afraid of him.

Bea would like to tell Jacob about her childhood holidays, about the singing aunt who had dressed her in clothes donated to the Protestant relief organisation – but perhaps Jacob would just find it boring.

He starts talking before she does, anyway, asking if she knows the story of Martha Liebermann. Her husband died at just the right time, one might say, in 1935, and his widow went on living in Berlin, in the beautiful large apartment on the Graf-Spee-Strasse which was a meeting place for artists and scientists, a thorn in the flesh for the Nazis: after all, not only was Liebermann Jewish, but already in 1933 he had announced his resignation from the Prussian Academy of Fine Arts. His widow, strange though it may sound, did not consider emigrating, and 'devoted herself' to the mistake – she belonged at all costs to the city which her family had lived in for hundreds of years, to the home of urbane liberalism. It was now just a question of keeping calm; reason and justice would triumph in the end. As her life became restricted by increasingly insidious measures – no more visits to the theatre, to concerts or to exhibitions, no wireless, no private telephone, no cheque-book – she felt humiliated, but to leave her home, the apartment she loved, her husband's grave in the cemetery on the Schönhauser Allee – she was simply unable to do it: she would rather accept having to wear the yellow star. Jacob says that his father knew her, he was an antiques dealer and had been able secretly to sell furniture and paintings belonging to the Liebermanns to help the impoverished widow. He never knew she committed suicide. Incidentally, Jacob's father left him and his mother in 1941.

Bea asks how long Jacob's father stayed in Berlin; he waves a hand dismissively and says, 'Oh him, far too long. He could have emigrated but he stayed in his beloved Fatherland, he couldn't stop being a German – a real German, not a German Jew, not a half-German – he was even a member of the Reichsbund of Jewish Front-Line Soldiers, and of the Association of Nationalist German Jews. His own parents were patriotic Germans, loyal to the emperor, they believed that Jewish people should be totally assimilated.' Jacob says, 'My mother's brother in Switzerland, where I was taken after the war, was contemptuous of my father, he called him an unbeliever. He was convinced his foolish brother-in-law in Berlin would have worn his Iron Cross, First Class – which he was awarded in 1917 for especial bravery – next to the yellow star on his coat lapel when he was being deported, hoping like a fool that volunteers who had served on the front in the First World War would somehow be spared.'

Jacob says, 'In May they read out the names in the Wittenbergplatz of fifty-five thousand Berlin Jews who were murdered. I didn't go to hear it, Heinrich Kluge was there. After eight hours they had only reached the letter J for Jacob. By the time they reached S for Stern, Kluge wasn't there any longer. He left because radical right-wing young people, among them pupils from your school, were singing their ghastly song.'

Jacob draws Bea away from Liebermann's *Girl in the Field*. He needs air. They pass through the galleries without stopping to stand in front of any more of the paintings; they lose their way, coming to rooms bristling with weapons, to rooms full of precious Gobelins. Bea would like to have a closer look at the woven battlefields, the landscapes and the courtly love scenes, but Jacob wants to get outside. The icy wind assails her. The wind is the worst thing here. Or are the half-starved children begging in the streets the worst? Or is it the beetroot-coloured borsch which gets stuck, like the word itself, between the teeth, which dyes one's urine blood red and the mere smell of which makes one nauseous?

In the Hotel Moskva, borsch is right at the top of the menu; nothing else on the menu is available any more, unfortunately sir and madam came in to dinner far too late.

They will have to find a restaurant offering something a bit tastier. Jacob doesn't want to take a taxi, he thinks the clear winter air will do him good. As they walk in a snow flurry through the streets looking for a restaurant, bracing themselves against the cruel wind, gloved hands stuffed right down into their coat pockets, St Petersburg is Leningrad again and they are Joseph Brodsky's elderly parents, shuffling from one state chancellery to the next, from one ministry to another in the hope of obtaining a travel permit before they died so they could visit their son who had been banished to America, and over a period of twelve years being told repeatedly that the government considered such a visit to be 'unpurposeful'.

They sit opposite one another in a pleasantly warm restaurant and confess that they had both thought of Brodsky's parents – two minds, with but a single thought, says Jacob, shaking his head; it is as though the poet is sitting with them at the table. Living in South Hadley, in America, Brodsky could only remember his parents in English, because it was in Russian that it had happened, that these two people had been taken away from him and so routinely destroyed. No country, he writes, has mastered the art of destroying its subjects' souls as well as Russia.

A friendly waitress serves them hot green tea, crisp, warm little pastry envelopes and flat dough cakes filled with fish, cabbage and mushrooms, called *pirozhki*, which are delicious. The manager of the restaurant comes up to their table and enquires whether everything has been to his esteemed guests' liking. They are obviously tourists, carrying foreign currency, so he offers to arrange for a horse-drawn sleigh to take madam and sir back to their hotel, wrapped up warmly with rugs.

A sleigh ride calls for jingling sleigh bells. The bell

around the horse's neck does not jingle; the clapper is probably iced over. So, quietly, they glide through the streets of St Petersburg, and the city is no longer Brodsky's Leningrad, with its façades pock-marked by bullets and shrapnel, nor is it the city encircled and bombarded by the German army, where over 650,000 people froze and starved to death, and which Bea's father could see through his binocular periscope. St Petersburg would be a resurrected city if one could ignore the muffled-up figures of the women and children begging on the pavements, and the occasional sledge laden with wood and twigs, leaving deep trails in the snow.

The sleigh driver uses his whip to point out the various sights, or at least those which he considers worth seeing, an especially beautiful Jugendstil façade, or magnificent, crumbling villas. As they pass the kilometres of arcades, the whip stays up in the air, pointing. Bea feels depressed by the imperial statement of the palaces and government buildings, before which people seem insignificant and weak. This architecture makes the winter even colder.

They go over one bridge and back again over another. The sleigh driver makes detours to show his passengers the stone river gods and sirens, a Samson tearing open the jaws of the lion, its coat decorated with extraordinary ice patterns, and the shadow of the whole splendid sculpture stretching out again plum coloured on the snow beneath. Soon the branching street lamps will light up, the cast-iron twin-headed Romanov eagle flying above them. The sky is still touched with pink; everywhere the light finds places to be reflected, glints on every surface, every dome. They could have driven over the Neva, too, for it has formed a bridge of ice. It looks as though the river is still, but beneath the frozen surface the water streams towards the Baltic. On the whiteness, silhouetted children throw snowballs at each other. Snowmen stand frozen along the river bank. At sixty degrees latitude, the feeble northern sun will not melt them.

Bea and Jacob watch everything from narrow observation slits: they have pulled their hats down over their foreheads and are holding their scarves pressed against their noses and mouths. When they lift their scarves to speak, their breath hangs in the air. Now and then the sleigh driver turns round and tells them something, but his words are mostly lost in the wind. They hear 'Stalin' and 'monument'; with a crack of his whip against the coachbox he makes them understand that all monuments to Stalin have disappeared. In their brochure it says that the bronze monuments have been melted down. The bronze from which one larger-than-life-size statue of Stalin had been cast, was shipped to Sweden so the Swedes could use it to make a bronze statue of Gustav Adolf, the original of which Stalin had stolen. In the former Leningrad, stone monuments had all been pulled down.

As a finale to the freezing sleigh ride, the coachman drives them to the only anti-Stalin monument, which is an opening in the quay wall of one of the Neva's side canals, with a view onto the administration buildings of the secret service and the GPU prison with its notorious torture rooms.

They get down from the sleigh onto stiff, frozen legs. The coachman tries to scrape the snow with his whip from the copper plaque which has been sunk into the earth in front of the small window, but the snow is too hard. He curses in Russian and then in guttural German tells them about his father, who was a tram driver. During the worst years, he says, when his father went on the early shift, he would always take an old pair of trousers and a jacket with him, for it frequently happened that a worker would jump onto the tram still wearing his nightshirt, just a blanket clutched around him, because he had drunk too much vodka and had overslept. Had he arrived late for work, he would have been beaten or even shot, as a warning to all the other idlers. The coachman demonstrates with sweeping gestures how his father used to put the trousers and the jacket on over some man's nightshirt and then steer him off the tram at the right stop. The clothes were always returned. There, under the snow, it tells you in Russian and English the atrocities that were carried out under Stalin. The coachman spits on the snow, and helps his passengers back into the sleigh.

Bea would like to say to him: 'My mother was deported in 1945 to Karabash,' but then she would also have to say that her father was at the siege of Leningrad. She wants to wrap herself up again in her rug, but it has frozen stiff in the cold to the second rug. Jacob pulls them apart, which is rather like tearing a cloak in half, and asks the coachman to take them back to the hotel by the quickest and most direct route. Never in her life has Bea been so cold as on this St Petersburg sleigh ride.

Never in my life have I been as cold as I was in Karabash. But who should I tell? Outside the cold and in the steelworks the heat. One after the other. This, then that. We all looked about seventy. Ruined skin. Our hair had grown back but it kept falling out again. Sometimes Boris had a Russian newspaper. He told us it said that in Germany all the Nazi leaders would be hanged. Of course the lady curate believed every word he said. I didn't. She told us that she never used to say 'Heil Hitler'. Whenever someone said Heil Hitler to her, she just said 'Heil him yourself!' a bit quietly of course, so they couldn't really hear what she was saying.

You can easily imagine her doing that. Once we had to scrub out both the latrines. Then she said we had come to Hell from another life but that other people had been living in Hell while we had been enjoying a good life. Or something like that, I wanted to try to remember the sentence exactly. In Karabash I couldn't stand the woman. She stood by the window in the hut. She stretched forward her right arm like a Hitler salute and then she said, 'The snow is <u>this</u> high!' In Germany she would have been sent straight off to a concentration camp for doing that. Just women who were ill, they were the only ones she did anything for. Hats off to her. Everyone else only thought about themselves. You *couldn't afford to be sorry for anyone. I had to stay on good terms with the lady curate so she'd take me to the sick hut.*

The German doctor there turned a blind eye as well. I just always had to tie something over my mouth and not touch anything. The doctor was wonderful. She wasn't at all afraid of catching something and did everything she could to help the women. Ruth said, she is an angel here in Hell. The Russians respected her too. They never came into the sick hut, they were terribly afraid of catching something. I've no idea how the doctor stood it. Day and night. The worst thing was the stink. You could always tell who had cholera, their eyes went very green. And people with jaundice had yellow ones. I don't know exactly what Ruth had. At the end she didn't want to eat any more. Just to drink all the time because of her fever. She couldn't look at me properly any more, her eyes kept sliding away. I knew her parents' address by heart. But Ruth thought they weren't alive any more. Not the child, either, because Berlin had been so heavily bombed. Ruth didn't want to go on. I would have given my soup away to have been able to help her.

When Jacob answered Bea's question about his father so succinctly, it meant that yet again she lost the opportunity to tell him about her own father, a lance-corporal of the Wehrmacht who from January to April 1943 was deployed with his unit – or does one say dug in? – before Leningrad. But Bea would not have begun her account with, 'Oh, him . . .' Jacob is ashamed of his father because he was more German than the Germans, so completely assimilated that he was embarrassed to be Jewish, adopting a sort of camouflage, part of which was the uniform of the active service volunteer, and the Iron Cross.

Bea need not feel ashamed of her father. She is lucky that he was a humble lance-corporal in an infantry regiment and not the commander in charge of the siege of Leningrad. Her father was not in charge of anything. But even if he had been, and even if she had not had such an unrealistic mother, who in February 1945 still wanted to go to a military hospital beyond Hinterpommern – if Bea were, for instance, the daughter of the letter-writer Hildegard Hiller, who ideally would have liked to change the first 'l' in her surname into a 't', would she then have had to feel ashamed, ashamed in front of Jacob for what her parents had done or not done before she was born, or at the time she was born?

Yes, she was lucky with her father.

Just a short field service letter today, he wrote on 13 November 1943, to Bea's mother. *On the orders of the Führer, all dispensable personnel have been withdrawn from the* Heeresgruppe Mitte *to join up with the* Heeresgruppe Nord. *I belong to the dispensable personnel who have ended up in the north. My postal number has not changed. We just have to change our watches here, two hours forwards. I would*

much rather be visiting Dostoevsky's grave in a city at
peace than shivering with the cold here. Or the
Hermitage. Or St Isaac's Cathedral. Since when do you
know how to knit? I am wearing your wonderful gloves
under my mittens. I will enclose another parcel stamp in
my next letter. Most important is to send tobacco, please,
as much as you can get hold of. I am clinging to my
pipe here. Look after yourself till the baby is born,
meine Herzallerliebste, *and stop carrying those heavy*
buckets of coal . . .

Are there words in other languages equivalent to
Herzallerliebste? Darling, *chérie, mon amour, amore, amore
carissimo*? How would one say it in Russian? Bea's
father had a lot of pet names for his bride and then for
his wife, and Bea's mother kept every one of his
letters, numbered and tied up in bundles, six hundred
and forty-eight of them, pale-blue field service letters
mostly, which were folded and sent unfranked, just
stamped with the word: FELDPOST. The date. The
German eagle. The faded grey-green envelopes containing the more detailed letters are adorned with a
mauve twenty-pfennig stamp showing Hitler's profile.

Her father seems to have given astonishingly little
thought to the censor; sometimes he expresses his
opinion in no uncertain terms: 'If only one knew how
to escape from this grindstone,' or, 'The last thing I
would want is the Order of Merit for Freezing in this
insane winter.'

Bea did not just come across the bundles of letters

in the attic after her grandparents died. Grandmother gave them to her, shortly before Bea was married. Her embarrassed smile said, 'But it was completely different for your parents, after all . . .'

What an awkward dowry that was, which she gave to Bea. From every man she liked, Bea expected the impossible. No wonder her marriage was doomed from the start, never mind the affair or two she had later on – they hardly deserved the word 'relationship' – affairs with nice, unloving lovers. Her grandmother would have done better to keep the letters to herself.

Bea had dreamed up parents to whom she could have meant everything, young, happy parents whom one could trust in good times and bad – though after the war they were more bad than good; chums, fairy-tale parents against whom Grandmother and Grandfather did not stand a chance. Bea must have made their lives very difficult – but how, actually? Her recollection of herself is of a lively, pleasant child. Though, of course, the pictures we have of ourselves are usually touched up. One of her aunts used to maintain that Bea was a child one's fingers itched to slap, a child who did not deserve her grandparents' patience. On another occasion she said that Bea's mother would turn in her grave if she could see how the child behaved.

Bea's mother should have seen how she played 'Dornröschen war ein schönes Kind, schönes Kind' – the story of the Sleeping Beauty – with the other children. She sang at the top of her voice, but only when she could be the Sleeping Beauty and sit in the middle of the circle, otherwise she would run off in tears. Bea's mother should have seen the family outing they all went on to Krummelanke. Bea had run on ahead as far as the inn, the only one which was open, burst into the bar, scrambled goodness knows how onto the counter, turned on the beer tap and sat there pleased as Punch as the frothing beer spurted out, streaming over the clear surface and onto the floor.

Bea does not recognise herself any more in the bubbly, boisterous child and is amazed how little impetuousness and unpredictability she has left. Baffled, she thinks herself back into the child who turned on the beer tap. Can that really have been her? So headstrong, a child for whom no tree, no counter was too high; a little girl who would only play if she could be the Sleeping Beauty, or the princess in the game of robbers they used to play in the devastated Grunewald forest. A granddaughter whose grandparents never knew what would happen next and who always got her own way, whether it was not eating up what was on her plate or not having to wear the clothes donated to the Protestant relief organisation. Grandfather would sigh and call her a stubborn rascal, and kiss her forehead. He would not recognise her nowadays. She doesn't even go cycling or swimming any more, if Jacob would rather not. She would love to take an icon from St Petersburg back with her: she would pay a lot of money for a genuine one, painted on wood and coated with varnish to preserve it – but she already knows that she won't buy one, or maybe only secretly, because otherwise she might have to explain to Jacob why an icon is more than just a souvenir for her.

Should Bea blame her unhappy marriage for the loss of her ability to assert herself? Straight after her final school exams, her favourite schoolteacher had married her. A sentence which must stay exactly the way it is. Her husband used to call her 'my child'. Even when she was expecting a child herself, he still called her his child – no, then he called her 'my dear Beate'. One Sunday morning, Bea laid the table with the beautiful gilt-edged breakfast service, the Royal Factory one, as though the revelation that she was pregnant would sound more credible within a festive context. 'We're expecting a baby. Isn't that wonderful?' Or did she say, 'What do you think about that?' His reaction was succinct and menacing: 'No children for five years, my dear Beate!' An unequivocal movement of the arm and outstretched hand over the table: I'll deal with this. I'll take it in hand. On that Sunday morning, Bea started to love the threatened child in her belly; she suddenly became a mother, a cat who rescues her kitten from the flames and singes her fur in doing so. While her husband took the matter in hand on the Monday, dealing with it in his way, she packed her things and moved back into her childhood bedroom.

Grandmother, who right from the start had prophesied that nothing good could come of the marriage, behaved as though she had never been away. And the child? The child would be fine, she promised; now life was returning to the house, now it was almost like at the end of the war again, when Bea's mother had been expecting her child. Everything they would need was already there and just had to be made ready: the cot, the little bath, the baby things; the little one could be weighed on the kitchen scales, just as they had weighed Bea. Grandmother rolled up her sleeves: this called for a proper spring-cleaning. She polished the red tiles in the hall as though important visitors were coming. The doorbell rang. Through the kitchen window Bea saw her husband take a few steps back from the front door and stand peering up at her bedroom window. Did he somehow imagine that he could fetch her back? She ran from the kitchen and through the hall and slipped, banging the back of her head so hard that she came to lying in a hospital bed. Concussion, badly broken right ankle joint, miscarriage of the foetus. A foetus in the fourth month of pregnancy is not a child; it does not get a burial. No grave. No funeral service. But a year of mourning.

Bea recovered from the effects of her broken ankle quicker than from the loss of her child. Its not being born. She hobbled into her university education on two crutches. Even now, past the menopause, she thinks about the child she could have had, sees the uncompromising gesture of the arm across the breakfast table: I'll deal with this. Apart from at the divorce,

Bea never again saw the man who announced that he would take it in hand.

It must have been completely different for her parents. In those days there were no endless discussions about whether one could afford a child, there was no economic miracle and one did not worry about one's career. And there was barely even the opportunity to make mistakes. There was the war being fought on land, at sea, in the air and on the news programmes, excerpts from which Bea watches with her pupils. There was the front and the home front and the longing of loved ones who had been torn apart. There was the field postal service, home leave and leave to get married – and then once again the longing which, as everyone knows, increases, squared by the distance.

Maybe even Bea's marriage would have been all right for a few years during the exceptional circumstances of the war, though only with difficulty can she imagine him calling her his *Herzallerliebste*, it would probably have stayed as 'my child'. Perhaps her husband would have been one of those men for whom the war was the ultimate adventure, eclipsing everything else, one of those who discover their leadership qualities through giving commands and exercising power. A uniform would have suited him splendidly, copiously decorated, of course. Only because Bea was still half a child could she have allowed herself to be married by her schoolteacher.

In the black-and-white photographs Bea's father looks like someone in fancy dress in his uniform, like

an extra in a war film. On 1 December 1943 he wrote
to Bea's mother:

*I am by nature such a private person, a snail which can
withdraw into its shell whenever it wishes. It is amazing
that they have somehow managed to cobble me into the
army, when I hate all that military lingo. If Sergeant
Möller could read my thoughts he would shout even
louder than he does already. Hey you, four-eyes! is how
he begins each sentence he addresses to me. But do not
worry, my treasure, I will struggle on. What is far more
important than my quarrels is that you should all stay
safe during the air-raids. They have evacuated so many
women and children from Berlin. You think you are safe
in Grunewald, as though your house were an
impregnable castle. Promise me that you will all go into
the shelter when the sirens start! I implore you, promise
me. You owe it to the little one, too. I know I
reinforced your cellar, but it only has one exit and it
could well happen that the water pipes get damaged . . .*

In another letter he writes:

*When I had to leave yesterday it almost broke my heart.
You are not allowed to accompany me to the railway
station in future. Saying goodbye like that is too terrible.
As the train drew away I could see you standing there,
the clouds of steam from the engine covering first your
legs, then your body, then your face, then your shining*

hair, so that I saw you not just getting smaller but also being cut into pieces. When the smoke faded I could not recognise you any longer amongst the mass of people on the platform.

The first days after we part are always the worst, for then I cannot imagine how I am going to prepare and steel myself, and get used to all the tedium again. I still have the sound of your sweet voice in my ears, my face is still buried in your hair. All my frailties can rest against you and my vulnerability is sheltered by you . . .

Bea will not show Jacob her father's letters to her mother, they should be seen by no one, not even by the daughter (though Bea reads them as though each line were addressed to her). If Jacob knew, he would surely ask: 'Father? Mother? But you never actually used those words. Parents from hearsay. You can't make up a story out of what you have never known.'

Christmas is everywhere, even in St Petersburg. In the hotel lobby stands a gaily decorated Christmas tree which reaches up to the ceiling. The women in Karabash also had a little Christmas tree.

Boris even got candles. And in the evening he gave us new blankets. They were as heavy and rough as the horse blankets at home. But clean. Then everyone got a big bar of washing soap and a small bar of chocolate.

Boris did it in a very festive way. He said spasi vas Gospodi *to everyone. And most of the women said* spasibo. *That means thank you in Russian. But I said thank you in German. Just don't start feeling at home here! Then we all sang 'Silent Night'. The brigade leader sang as well. Boris knew the song too. He sang it in Russian. He really belted it out because he was already drunk. I just opened and shut my mouth. The brigade leader said she knew for sure that the camp would soon be closed. First the sick ones would be freed, then the others.* Damoy. Home. *We believed it of course. Ruth was already in the sick hut. The lady curate was thin as a rake and looked like a ghost too. But she kept going, and visited the sick.*

On the afternoon of the twenty-fourth, when they return from the Hermitage, where Jacob finally inspected the finds from the Altai frost-graves, Bea goes into town alone under the pretext of getting something from the chemist's. She wants to buy Jacob a present. Even if they cannot celebrate Christmas together she would like to do something to please him.

Searching for interesting-looking junk shops in the old part of the city, she passes through narrow little alleyways, criss-crossed by dimly lit, frozen canals. The snow has been swept to one side and reaches to the low windows of the houses. Somewhere here, Dostoevsky's Raskolnikov must have lived in his attic, in a tiny yellow room *which felt like a cupboard*. He stole through these alleyways on one of those white summer nights, a hatchet hidden beneath his coat, to kill the usurer, Alena Ivanovna, and her sister Elisaveta.

As tourists rarely wander around here, you do not come across women or children begging. They start to pester you again on the Nevsky Prospekt, near the brightly illuminated shop windows where the world's luxury is on display: Italian shoes, high boots and ankle boots, French perfumes, Spanish wines and kosher wines from Israel, and everywhere the precious porcelain of the Imperial Porcelain factory of St Petersburg, dinner services and tea services with delicate garlands of flowers, cobalt-blue rims and the portrait of Catherine the Great. In the window of one antique shop are roulette wheels of every size, the slots inlaid with ebony or onyx and red lacquer, ivory balls to decide one's fate. Should Bea give Jacob a small roulette wheel as a gift?

A cheeky boy plucks at her coat until she gives him a ruble, but even then he does not stop. She takes refuge in a bookshop; perhaps she will find something for Jacob here. Doing something to please him is not easy. She is rarely able to read his wishes in his eyes. He claims not to have any wishes, for one wish will always be replaced by another. He once called himself a spoilt ascetic. He loathes everything he does not absolutely need.

Nevertheless, since she knows how much he loves Chekhov, she buys a lavishly illustrated biography, the text printed in German, English and Russian. They wrap the book for her in Christmassy paper and fasten a fir twig on the top. Back on the street an old man is hawking Russian dolls: '*Matrioshki, matrioshki!* Buy, pretty lady!'

So she buys a Russian doll too, and only later that evening, as they are exchanging gifts in the hotel room, does she notice that the dolls, which fit one inside the other, have the faces of Russian revolutionaries and heads of state: the outside one is clearly Yeltsin, bloated, with a double chin; beneath him, unmistakable owing to the birthmark on his forehead, Gorbachev. After that, the next one to emerge is a grumpy-looking face with thick black eyebrows – is it Khrushchev? Or Brezhnev? Under him squats a wooden Stalin with moustache and pipe and, last of all, a tiny Lenin. In the place where a medal would go, on his breast, he wears the year 1917. So, there the five busts stand, in a row, arranged according to size, and not just one row: Jacob was also persuaded to buy a Russian doll – '*Matrioshki, matrioshki!* Buy, nice gentleman!' – and he bought three at once, one for Bea, one for his friend Kurz, and a third one, fatter, almost as big as the other two together, for one of the thirty-six just men, as he mysteriously says.

Jacob bought the dolls from a woman, and when he took three she shrieked a blessing, *spasi vas Gospodi!* and made the sign of the cross over him, so that, what with the shock and the embarrassment, he almost dropped the precious gift he had just bought Bea and which he now presents to her along with the doll and a fir twig: an icon, exactly the sort Bea would have bought herself, a St George, preparing to throw his lance to slay the monstrous dragon lying at the feet of his white horse.

Bea's eyes grow moist with pleasure. Jacob is familiar with this, he calls her a first-class weeper. He takes her in his arms and kisses away her tears of happiness; it takes a while as she is at this moment the happiest person in the whole of St Petersburg. Between kisses, Jacob tells her, and he is not being ironic, that St George protects against all evil and that this picture was not painted by human hand, the art dealer gave him his assurance.

They order some red wine, a Rothschild, to be brought up to their room and a cold dish with chicken drumsticks, breast of veal and anchovy filets, garnished with mustard seeds, pickled cucumbers and onions, carrots, parsley and radishes. A hot green sauce is served with it, once again bringing tears to the eyes. After the meal Jacob orders a bottle of champagne, which is brought along with two beautifully engraved goblets, a crystal bowl with nuts and pretzel sticks, and a crystal candelabrum. The room-service waiter lights the candles and says, '*Spasi vas Gospodi*'; his left arm held against his back, he makes such a deep bow that he almost loses his balance, and one can see in the extravagance of the gesture the generosity of the tip Jacob has slipped him. When the waiter wheels the trolley out of the room an hour later, Jacob holds the door open for him and helps himself to the leftover radishes from the otherwise empty dish. 'Spasi vas Gospodi,' says the waiter, bowing, 'spasi vas Gospodi.'

'Do you know what that means?' asks Jacob.

'It's a sort of blessing, something like God be with you.'

'You're already speaking Russian in your sleep,' says Jacob. 'This morning just before you woke up you said "proverke" a few times, or "proserke". What does that mean?'

' "Provertje" means count, or check. Did I really say that?'

'How else would I know the word? What were you dreaming about?'

'I've forgotten. But it can't have been a very pleasant dream if I said provertje.'

Jacob turns a radish on its stalk this way and that, looking at it as though he has never seen a radish before. 'Do you like radishes?'

'Goodness me – yes, what makes you ask?'

'I just wondered.' Jacob sets the wooden dolls out on the wicker table, a whole cast of Yeltsins, Gorbachevs, Khrushchevs or Brezhnevs, Stalins and Lenins. Bea shows off how well she can draw, using a ball-point pen, lipstick and nail varnish to transform one of the twin Stalins into a Chaplinesque Hitler, with a toothbrush moustache right up under the nose and a quiff over the forehead. Turning Khrushchev, or Brezhnev, with his round head into Hermann Goering is easy: pull the corners of the mouth up into a smile in the doughy face, put a royal stag's antlers on him and suggest an array of medals and decorations on the breast. Then she removes the beard of one small Lenin, opens his mouth and draws deep lines round it, and parts his hair exactly, so it looks just like Goebbels. She does not make Gorby or Yeltsin up to look like anyone else: all such comparisons are inappropriate and distort history.

Jacob unscrews the dolls and fits them together again, and moves their heads around so that their ties, their insignia of power, hammers and sickles, slip onto their backs. Bea builds a pyramid out of the largest dolls, on which Stalin's beard and pipe and Gorby's birthmark are as big as the smallest Lenin. Jacob suggests making a paper chessboard and playing a game using the dolls as pieces but Bea has never learnt how to play and, in any case, the champagne has gone to her head. Jacob pours the rest of the bottle into two of the lower halves of the wooden dolls and vows never again to mix heavy red wine and champagne.

He opens the book that Bea gave him and reads aloud from Chekhov's diary, where he writes that although there is more Russian lethargy than courage in him, he went to Sakhalin, to the place of unbearable suffering. He even witnessed a whipping, but everyone in Russia and the rest of the world denied that it was any concern of theirs. 'God's world is beautiful, only one thing is not beautiful: we are not.' Jacob shuts the book and draws Bea onto his lap, afraid the tears might start again.

His mouth close to her ear, he tells her that the largest wooden doll is intended for an old man in Cherbourg, who, as a prisoner of war, worked in a market garden and nursery in Klein-Machnov. The nursery still exists, the house, the yard, the hothouses, everything is still there, even prettier than before, the house freshly decorated, with a terrace built on, the hothouses modernised: they use plastic panes nowadays instead of glass, and there are three 'warm houses' with supplementary ventilation.

Bea is uncomfortable on Jacob's lap but she tries to sit lightly and does not move because she is afraid that Jacob's ingrained habit of silence might make him stop talking. He is not going to give her a lecture on hothouses now, he is going to talk about the child who hid in one.

'Hidden in a hothouse,' her colleague Kurz said; 'as far as I know, they hid Jacob in a hothouse.'

Bea has often wondered who 'they' could have been. Of course, she has heard and read that there were certainly some Germans who risked their lives by hiding Jews in cellars, in attics with false walls, in all sorts of strange places; or who smuggled Jewish children, who were not supposed even to exist any more, into their own families, and had to fabricate stories full of lies and win over a cast of supporting actors so they could keep their rescue operations going. Even so, she has never actually met anyone who risked his own life in order to protect someone who was ruthlessly being persecuted by the dictators. Were these rescuers supermen, saints, heroes? Was it self-evident to them that they must help? Was it impossible for them not to help, without any fuss or feelings of self-righteousness?

Jacob now starts talking about a woman, she was a cunning minx, a Berlin slut, who, as a so-called *Pflichtjahrmädel*, had to do her community service during the third year of the war in the nursery in Klein-Machnov. But it was not work she had in mind so much as the son of the owner of the nursery: she tricked him into marrying her, claiming that she was pregnant by him. What she really did was to marry into the business, to ingratiate herself and sneak in: she was not pregnant at all, something her very young husband never realised, as he fell somewhere on the fifteen-thousand-kilometre-long front which Germany had to defend. The young war widow made out that she had suffered a miscarriage, but her mother-in-law had seen through her long before and did not believe a word. A war broke out between the two, just as relentless as that which their country was fighting. The older woman worked hard and mourned her only son; the younger one was hopeless both in the flower shop and at making wreaths, she could just about manage the weeding, and even then one had to watch out that she did not pull the wrong green bits out of the earth. What she did in her free time, the mother-in-law preferred not to know.

Jacob's mother knew both women by sight. She lived very near the nursery and often, when she was passing, she looked covetously into the hothouses. During the war, they mostly grew vegetables there, radishes, tomatoes, kohlrabi, cucumbers and lettuce, delicacies to which Jews were not entitled; what they were allowed to buy in certain shops between four and five o'clock in the afternoon was too little to live and too much to die. So Jacob's mother sometimes plucked up the courage to go into the garden and beg a few radishes, apples or potatoes. The young woman was good-natured and occasionally gave her something.

Jacob moves Bea back onto her wicker chair. She is getting too heavy for him. Now he must go on with what he was saying. He cannot start and then just stop talking. Bea takes care not to let him sense how eager she is to hear what he will say next. In front of her on the tabletop, St George leans far back, aiming his lance into the dragon's fiery jaws. Bea will hang the icon with the other pictures in her bedroom, on the light-filled wall she looks at when she wakes up in the morning. And in case there should ever again be a time without Jacob, she will think of this St Petersburg Christmas Eve, every detail of it: the wooden dolls whose heads Jacob twisted round and out of which they drank champagne; the candles in the crystal candelabrum and the room-service waiter who made such a low bow; her tears of joy which Jacob kissed away – a picture which will never fade; the creaky wicker chair and the bed which did not creak; Jacob's mouth, the scent of pipe tobacco and above all Jacob's voice; words like *too little to live and too much to die*, uttered almost casually . . . For heaven's sake, she must defend herself against this sort of premature reminiscing!

Jacob fills his pipe again and looks closely at St George, who is supposed to protect against all evil.

This morning, he asked Bea if she would like to go to church; he wouldn't have anything against it, he is even envious that she belongs to a religion while he always has to put a line after the word 'religion' when he is filling out forms. He is just stubborn, he says. Lovely for her to be able to believe in something, but then of course maybe she believes for the sake of believing in something. She let him speak and, silently and without moving her lips, sang *Oh, Heiland reiss den Himmel auf*, because she sings it every year and because her mother sang it in Karabash, in Hell.

On Christmas Eve it didn't work out with the sick hut. The lady curate couldn't take me in with her. But she could on Christmas Day. The women told us they had been given things too. Chocolate and soap and all the same men's nightshirts. I brought Ruth half my chocolate. I told her it was from the whole hut. She was so pleased. I also told her we would soon be freed, the sick ones first of course. And that we'd certainly be allowed to write home soon.

The women said they wanted to sing again. Everyone could choose a song, like on a musical request programme. Ruth wanted Oh, Heiland reiss den Himmel auf, *but the others only knew the first verse. Ruth sang the rest. But it was more like mumbling. You couldn't understand it very well. Then she said, 'Tell me about your sister. She was only fifteen, I'm sure they let her go straight away, in Quakenburg, I'm sure you'll see her again.' But then Ruth fell asleep. She said she was always so tired.*

Then she woke up again. She asked me, 'Do you still remember my address?' I said, 'Yes, of course, Berlin-Grunewald, Rotwildpfad 4.' I asked if she still knew mine. 'Yes, of course,' she said, 'Hohenneuendorf, near Bromberg. But there isn't anyone left of your family, you know.' She said that. When she was feverish. You have to remember that.

This is just what Bea must not remember for the hundredth time. Especially not today. She moves round the *matrioshki*, the St Petersburg version of the figures in the manger, stands them in a circle around the edge of the wicker table and then makes them march off in formation, the biggest at the front. Count. *Provertje*. The leftover champagne has become warm, the bubbles have turned to pearls in the wooden dolls. Jacob drains his cup and rolls a radish between his thumb and forefinger. Bea can picture what Jacob now tells her as if she were watching a television film.

One day, Jacob's mother ventured into the nursery around closing time, to see if she could get hold of a bunch of carrots or radishes, or a lettuce. As she crept through the extensive grounds, she saw through the glass wall of a hothouse, right in the furthest corner where boxes, flower pots and turf were piled up, the young gardener's wife tearing off her clothes and hurriedly having sex with the French prisoner of war.

'He was called Auguste,' says Jacob, 'and he was a gardener by profession. The young woman was called Berta. Auguste always called her "Erta", with the stress on the "a". Ertá.'

Bea can guess what is coming next. If she had been Jacob's mother she too would have used what she knew to blackmail this Berta: if German women had sexual contact with prisoners of war they could face the death penalty. Jacob's mother's situation was desperate; yes, she went to the young woman and told her what she had seen, and threatened to report her to the authorities unless a bag of vegetables, fruit and potatoes was hung twice a week in a certain place on the garden fence for her; she had a child, a little boy, who would otherwise go hungry.

Had she already considered where the blackmail could lead? On the day that she would be rounded up and taken away to Grunewald railway station, she took her child to Berta, or rather not so much to her as to her lover, the French prisoner of war, Auguste, who had given her the vegetables a few times. She gave them all her jewellery and begged them to hide her son, in a shed or under the long table in a greenhouse, so he would not be cold. Not for long; the war could not go on for months, just a few weeks at the most. She blackmailed them, threatening that she would report them even from the labour camp.

Jacob has got into his stride now. He hardly pauses for breath, as though the whole thing must be told once and for all, before the memory is irretrievably smoothed over by time. As Bea listens to him, it is as though she has once again broken the seal of a long-hidden letter.

Jacob says, 'My mother went down on her knees before them, Auguste told me when I visited him twenty years later in Cherbourg to thank him. But he didn't want thanks. He said my mother had saved his life by keeping his secret and so he had saved my life. *C'est tout*. He'd forgotten almost all his German, but he still remembered that my mother had stammered 'too kind' when he promised to hide me, 'too kind, Monsieur Auguste'. Auguste confessed to me then that he'd sold most of my mother's jewellery to fulfil his dream: he'd wanted to start a little circus, but it hadn't worked out; for a few years he was the clown in a big circus and could make people laugh. Since his time as a prisoner of war in Germany, he'd been put off gardening.'

Walking up and down the room, at first Jacob hardly mentions the little boy who sat there in the greenhouse and had to be invisible, the childhood that was snatched away from him, that piece of unlived life. But he describes in detail his visit to Cherbourg: Auguste had played down the whole story, as though it had been easy, hiding a child from the thugs for a year and a half. And indeed it hadn't been so hard at first. *Le petit Jacob* was a good boy and sat there quietly, because he thought – so they kept assuring him – that his mother would be coming to fetch him soon. Auguste himself assumed that the war would be over in a few weeks. At the time, after the Americans had already liberated Normandy and captured the German troops in his native city, he had thought they'd be in Berlin soon too, Pope Pius was praying for it every day. But although the Germans were fighting defensively, and were in retreat, and although entire armies had been surrounded in the east, the madness never came to an end.

'In the end,' says Jacob, 'Auguste tried to get me away by confiding in a French priest. Of course, he was a prisoner too, but he was allowed to look after his fellow Frenchmen. During the week, most of them were billeted with the people they worked for and at weekends a German sergeant would take them to their camps. But Auguste was released for work on

Sundays as well, because the nursery needed looking after and because the woman who owned it relied on his being there to help every day. Once a month Auguste was taken to mass and communion in the camp. There was no confessional. Things being as they were, it probably would have been fitted with a bugging device anyway.

'But Auguste was able to whisper to the abbé that there was a Jewish child who had to be smuggled out of Berlin and away from Germany, a boy, who unfortunately looked very Jewish. I remember they shut me up once in a big box with wood shavings inside, quickly packed me up like a fragile cherub which has to be dispatched somewhere, then I was driven around for a while on a bumpy wagon and finally unpacked again back in Auguste's wash-house. The abbé had wanted to get me on a transport of children arranged by a Dutch rescue organisation, but it had left without me. The box stayed in the courtyard for a long time. The other chance of getting me out of the country, this time with the Quakers' help, was lost because the person who would have come to collect me turned out to be unreliable. The abbé could only arrange these rescue attempts in absolute secrecy, and he had to rely on helpers, and helpers of helpers: if just one link of the chain was weak, the whole plan was abandoned, otherwise it could end in disaster. No one knew how long the war would go on and what would happen to them. It was a question of endurance, of changing one's plans every day. And it was a question of absolute fearlessness.'

Jacob says, 'I don't know if I would have been capable of risking my life for complete strangers in a similar situation.' He says, 'I couldn't vouch for myself.'

Bea has singed all the needles off the fir twigs. She waits patiently for Jacob to go on with the story.

He says, 'I didn't go hungry. I wasn't cold. I just had to be invisible. And I had to be quiet. Auguste made two hiding places for me, one in the hothouse which was furthest away from the house and the shop. I would creep behind piled-up sacks of turf and planks and under the wooden table which the plants stood on. It was a cramped little place and there were spiders with eight eyes and eight legs. But I only had to go into it when Auguste or Berta gave a warning whistle. Berta's mother-in-law stayed in the shop all day, or was busy in the house, and Auguste swore she had never set foot in his quarters, which used to be the wash-house. I remember it as being almost cosy in there. There was even a blue curtain hanging in front of the one high window. Auguste made me a little place on the old base of the boiler. He hung sacks, aprons and trousers around it and I used to sleep there. Auguste told me that he had walled my mother's jewellery into the fireplace beneath where I slept, so well hidden that the Gestapo would never be able to find it. Knowing that I was lying on top of my mother's jewellery comforted me when I went to bed and when I woke up.

'When the air-raid sirens went off in the night, Auguste was always there. The old woman would have let him go in her cellar but he never wanted to. On the outskirts of Berlin he felt safer in the open. My mother and I hadn't been allowed to go into any air-raid shelters apart from one cellar at the Teltower Damm which was reserved for Jews. It didn't have the letters LSR on the iron door leading to the *Luftschutzraum*, like on the doors of Aryan shelters. I think LSR were the first letters I could read, and to me they spelt: "You can't come in here." Auguste used to laugh and say, "LSR doesn't mean *Luftschutzraum*, it means *Lernt Schnell Russisch!* – learn Russian quickly!" '

Jacob says, 'Auguste managed to calm me when I shook with terror during the air-raids, probably because he wasn't in the least afraid himself. When I think of him now, he seems to have been like a tight-rope walker who performed without a net or like a clown with a painted laughing mouth. His face was like a clown's, and he could conjure crayons from his jacket sleeves, apples from his mouth. He could do all sorts of things: stand on his head, wiggle his ears, walk on his hands, pull faces, make birds out of pieces of cloth, imitate every bird call. Best of all, he could do ventriloquism. He'd say something without moving his lips and it sounded as though it was coming from somewhere completely different. I wanted to learn how to do it too, and Auguste tried his best to teach me. I practised for hours on end with him, breathing in deeply, dividing the air when I breathed out, and getting the muscles of my larynx to vibrate. I became a master ventriloquist – so don't be surprised if you hear a voice coming from somewhere. When there were daytime air-raids, Auguste would come running the minute the siren went off. Then he'd say, "Now you're safe, *petit Jacob*, the old lady's in the cellar." We'd sit down in the deep hollow that Auguste had dug and he'd cross himself and recite a prayer in French. He only ever prayed in French.

'I remember exactly what it was like when the bombers flew low overhead. The panes of glass in the hothouse behind our hollow would chirp like insects. On a clear day we could see the silver squadron and the vapour trails they left behind, and Auguste thought they should pass over again, because then the war would be over quicker and my mother would be able to come back from the labour camp and fetch me.'

Jacob says, 'I believed every word Auguste said.'

Now Bea interrupts him for the first time and says that she was born during one of those daytime raids over Berlin, maybe just as he sat in the hollow and . . .

Jacob pushes his glasses higher onto his nose with the forefinger of his right hand and gazes at her, as though he temporarily forgot she was there and has been talking to himself rather than to her. He says, 'Everything depended on the woman who owned the nursery, that she didn't become suspicious. But Berta was cunning. Auguste told me that because she was afraid of the authorities and of her mother-in-law, she'd become quite good at her work in the garden and the hothouses, just to keep the old woman busy in the shop and the house, but, he said, if she ever caught sight of me, I was to start crying and say I had run away from a children's home and had hidden there but that I'd quickly run back again. Then I was supposed to take to my heels and run, and hide somewhere till evening. And if the women who made the wreaths – because occasionally they worked in the nursery and then would use our earth closet – if they caught sight of me I was to tell them the same story. But Auguste always warned me when the women were about. Then I couldn't use the earth closet. I doubt whether I really could have pretended I was a runaway in an emergency: seven- or eight-year-old boys aren't very good actors. And why did I have to look so Jewish?

'Berta used to bring me my food in a mess tin, and always the same sort of fruit tea in an army canteen. My greyish-green sleeping bag had once belonged to the Wehrmacht, too. I wonder now how they managed to make me understand the reason why I had to stay hidden for so long. They must have drummed it into me that my mother had to be in a labour force, like all grown-up Jews. When the war was over – which would be soon, of course, very soon – yes, then, only then would my mother come to fetch me. I probably didn't doubt this explanation and I stayed quiet as a mouse. Or is it that in such extreme circumstances children suddenly become grown up and reasonable? How did I while away the time? Did I pester Auguste with questions? Did I cry a lot, wet my trousers? I think I was more afraid of the spiders than of being discovered or of the air-raids. I was waiting for my mother.

'Strangely enough, I don't remember being bored. Berta used to bring me books, picture books and colouring books, and toys which had belonged to her dead husband. I made both tatty books of fairy tales even tattier; I still know the *Struwwelpeter* off by heart. My favourite character was Flying Robert. There was the same primer my mother had used to teach me, with the same printing. Berta brought me a jumping jack who jerked his arms and legs up when you pulled the string. I thought it so stupid that I took it apart. There was a box of bricks, too, and the faces of the wooden blocks had pictures from fairy tales stuck on to them, but one block was missing. There was always that one block missing, so in Cinderella the step with the lost shoe wasn't there, and the Sleeping Beauty didn't have a head. So I carved a block of wood which fitted exactly into the gap, and I drew on each of the six faces to make the pictures complete.'

Jacob says, 'In Cherbourg, Auguste told me that the abbé had also tried to get me accepted by a church organisation for Christians of Jewish descent. I had to be prepared especially for it. Believe it or not, I eagerly learnt the prayers and liturgical phrases which Auguste taught me. He'd say, '*Allelujah!* and '*Oly, 'oly, 'oly is the Lord,* and murmur the incomprehensible words, *Blessed be the fruit of thy womb.* I practised

132

kneeling and crossing myself so as to look convincing to the people from the organisation for Christians of Jewish descent. But it never actually got to that point because the abbé paid for his kindness with his life.

'The ways in which people who had been lured by the Gestapo to become informers operated, in a city of over a million inhabitants like Berlin, were sadly not so exactly documented as the post-war machinations of the East German State security service, where every movement of both the guards and the guarded was put on record. Did you see on television those rows of sacks, full of shredded Stasi files? It's a macabre puzzle, and by the year 2010 it should be pieced together.'

Jacob does not wait for Bea to answer. He goes on: 'One day, Auguste told me that the woman who owned the nursery had got herself a dog to guard the house and the grounds. He'd secretly had to poison it, otherwise it would have sniffed me out. He'd never harmed an animal before, and it was such a beautiful big dog . . . And then came a time when I had to stay nearly all day in my hiding places because refugee families from the east were staying in the house. The children used to play in the garden. I could hear them. Sometimes they rattled at the closed door of the washhouse or used the door as "home" for "Who's afraid of the big bad wolf?" No one! they all shouted. No one's afraid here.

'Had I learnt not to feel fear by repressing normal reactions to danger? Does one learn to fall into a sort of trance during the worst moments? To overcome fear by numbing the emotions? Looking back, I think I became a master at it, like at ventriloquism.'

Once upon a time there was a little boy. He lived in the most unjust country in the world. Is Jacob saying that, or did Brodsky write it?

'And then?' asks Bea. 'What happened then, when you were allowed to exist again?'

'Then the artillery explosions came nearer and nearer, the drone of low-flying aircraft louder and louder. And Hitler married and shot himself through the head, maybe he also swallowed poison, to be sure. I can easily imagine that despite the cyanide and the bullet it still took him a long time to die, like the demon Rasputin. And then, when he was dead at last, I could look Jewish again. Auguste gently broke the news to the nursery owner that he'd been hiding me the whole time, and he explained to her how grand she would appear now, at the end of the war, when it emerged that she'd been brave enough to save the life of a Jewish child.'

'And did she feel heroic?'

'She stared at me as if I were an apparition from another world. And I stared at all the furniture which was crammed into the living room. It was without any doubt our furniture, from our living room: the octagonal table which I used to play under, the dresser with the nicely turned columns, the long sideboard, even the rug with roses around the edge – Berta had probably gone to get the things as soon as my mother was taken away. Before Auguste left he entrusted me, not to the old woman or to Berta, but to a refugee from Danzig, who as soon as she saw me started sobbing and took me in her arms as though I was one of her own children.

'Auguste gave this woman some of my mother's jewellery and she promised to take me to a Jewish organisation or to Allied headquarters as soon as the situation in Berlin became a bit clearer. Auguste wanted to hand the rest of the jewellery over to me but I only took a pair of earrings which I had often seen my mother wear. And as for Berta, she disappeared, somewhere in Berlin, with all the chains and rings and brooches she had been given to keep me safe. I think she was probably one of those women who became involved with American soldiers, the ones who were called the *Fräuleinwunder*. Auguste hugged me when we said goodbye: "*Adieu, mon petit Jacob.*" He gave me his address. I think that was the last time I ever cried.

'All sorts of people hugged me in the weeks that followed. I stayed the whole summer at the nursery. I was supposed to sleep in the attic with a refugee boy, but I slept in Auguste's bed and I was generally there during the day too and didn't allow anyone into my kingdom. I hadn't learnt to play with other children. Once or twice the woman who owned the nursery showed me off to people I didn't know and boasted that she had saved my life. Should I have told them that the very opposite was true? At mealtimes she gave me twice as much to eat as the refugee children. Because of this they loathed me, and beat me up a few times. When the old woman found out she beat them

135

all black and blue until the other women intervened, but the old woman protected me: now she had her Jew to show off.

'In the house the women squabbled and shrieked the whole time. I retreated into my abode and bolted the door, or sat around in the hothouses.'

The candles have burnt right down. Bea waits a moment until she asks, 'And then?'

'Then? Then I was a displaced person again. The woman from Danzig took me to an UNRA camp for persons displaced at the time of Hitler. I never counted how many children slept there in just the one room, but we were two or three to a bed and we were hungry and cold. It was worse than it had ever been in the wash-house. Luckily I developed jaundice and was in hospital for a long time, where I had a bed with white sheets all to myself.'

Jacob says, 'It was a Catholic hospital. At Christmas the nuns built a manger and put almost life-size, colourful carved wooden figures in it, and sang carols about peace on earth. A lot of children got visitors. My mother didn't come. But my hopes hadn't faded. When I was allowed to get up, I looked out of the window and saw a snow-covered landscape of rubble. I still don't know whereabouts in Berlin the hospital was.

'In the spring of 1946 one of the nuns took me to Zurich to my mother's only brother. He was a jeweller, as my grandfather had been, and a strictly observant Jew, like his father. He had never forgiven his sister for marrying a non-believer. In his opinion my mother was a shiksa. I was welcomed into the family like a long-lost son – not one who gets an overwhelming greeting, they certainly didn't kill the fatted calf – more like one who has to be taught what a real Jew is. When my uncle blessed his children he'd bless me too, but never without reciting a fervent prayer over my head which I didn't understand.

'I didn't understand anything at all, not the readings from the Torah before mealtimes and not the stories that were told when the Chanukah candles were lit. At Chanukah the prayers and singing were very loud. My three cousins, who had sidelocks and wore yarmulkas, spoke Hebrew at home and otherwise Swiss German. I must have seemed like an alien to them, something from another planet. When we covered our eyes during the blessing at the Shabat meal, they peeped through their fingers to see if I was doing everything correctly. At such times, I'd remember my ventriloquism and produced swearwords which seemed to come from the door or through a window and gave everyone at the table a shock. No one could prove I'd said them because no word had passed my lips.

'Joshua was my age. He was already in the first year at the Jewish grammar school. Because I'd never been to school he thought I was stupid, and took every opportunity to show me. One Friday evening as we were coming out of synagogue, he said he had distinctly seen that I hadn't turned to the door to greet the Shabat bride, but then someone like me wouldn't see her anyway. Another time, on the way home from synagogue, he said that everyone who has properly prepared for Shabat is accompanied home by two angels, but they'd leave me to go home alone because I was twice lost, according to the scriptures.'

Jacob says, 'Are you surprised now that I don't keep any of the countless religious laws, don't keep Shabat, or the dietary laws? I eat meat with milk and my favourite food is pork dripping with crackling. I have nothing to do with any of them. I suspect that in your blue eyes I'm a Jew who's no longer Jewish, aren't I?'

He sits down heavily on the wicker chair and is silent for a long time. He looks older. He looks as if he has fallen asleep. Then at last he goes on, fiercely, 'Whatever. My uncle became my guardian, after we found out that my father had died directly after his return from God knows where, from the effects of having been in the concentration camp. And my mother? I have no idea if my uncle tried to find out where she was. Anyway, my uncle became my guardian. He had charge of me until my twenty-first birthday. He did his best – or let's say he honestly tried, but actions speak louder than words. He didn't once ask me about my life in Berlin, about the years with my mother and those without her in the nursery. In Zurich I was simply supposed to be what he wanted, just a Jew. And for that he had a complete education programme worked out. At first he even employed a tutor for me. Then the Jewish school. Ten years' brainwashing. Ten kosher years with gefilte fish and chicken soup. Fasting on Yom Kippur.

Ten years of lighting candles. But the extra soul that a religious Jew acquires didn't want to come to me. Ten years of Sukkoth to remember the time when my people lived in the wilderness, Pesach to remember the flight from Egypt, continually having to remember something which I couldn't remember.

'I know I'm unfair about my relatives in Zurich. They meant well. Their spiritual home was intact, even if everything had become routine and the grandmother's funeral was dealt with rather hastily because she died right in the middle of the Christmas rush. That splendid shop in town, with its four large windows, was the centre of my uncle's world. No one was allowed to go near him when he came home in the evening. It was obvious how tired he was. It never felt like my home, that big house with the lowered venetian blinds. I was an onlooker.

'Of course, I was often difficult. But it was only when I left school and wanted to go to study in Berlin that I lost my uncle's goodwill. He thought I was mad. I thought I was mad, too. It was incomprehensible. I wanted to go back to Berlin. Goodness knows why there . . .'

'You wanted to go to your wash-house. To your hothouse.'

'Dear God,' says Jacob. 'Did I want to piece together German fairy tales again? But I suppose it must have been some sort of rebirth.'

Before they go to sleep, Bea opens the windows to air the room. The icy cold sweeps in, bringing the sound of ringing bells. Pavlov's dog barks somewhere nearby. Bea sees a sky to which only the word firmament could really do justice, each star shining brighter than the next. On this Christmas night they lie very still next to each other, as though they are brother and sister, or mother and child, and as though the hours in which one of them opened up his heart are too precious for passion; as though nothing can transcend trust, and as though that were a better word for love.

The Russian winter bothers them more than they admit. Jacob no longer tries to hide his fear of catching colds and other infections. At mealtimes he now quite openly wipes the forks, the spoons and the rims of the cups and glasses with his napkin; he sees bacteria and viruses lurking everywhere. When Bea first met him, she thought his concern for his well-being was a symptom of his melancholy. Now she knows that he was a pampered child whose mother took excessive care of him to compensate for the danger he was in. For seven years he had nobody but this adoring mother, who for her son became father, brother, sister and playfellow rolled into one.

Kurz, Bea's colleague, encouraged her to cheer Jacob up a bit. Paradoxically, she finally manages it in a St Petersburg cemetery. After visiting Dostoevsky's grave in the Tikhvin cemetery, and laying a bunch of winter asters in front of the larger-than-life-size bust of the writer, they go to Mussorgsky's burial place. The thin layer of ice on the puddles is brittle and cracks underfoot but it does not break. Only the main paths have been swept. The saplings bend under the snow's weight; some have already snapped. Frozen blades of grass, studded with crystal, decorate the snow-covered graves. They have tears in their eyes, from the cold, the wind. Instead of shivering their way here they could have stayed nice and warm in Berlin. Is it now really necessary to pay their respects to the famous dead?

Jacob has his hip flask with him and takes a sip from time to time to warm himself. Just as he is taking the flask from his mouth, two policemen appear from a side path and shout, 'Here *nix spirtnoye*, nix schnapps, here *kladbishche*, here *pochtenie*, here piety!'

Gesturing, they are plainly telling Jacob that he has committed an offence with his flask and that he should please go with them. But the custodians of the law don't know Bea.

'*Nix* schnapps,' she cries indignantly, '*nix* spirit! It is mediciiine!' She draws out the 'i' so long that it lingers on her breath. 'Mediciiine! My husband *malade*,' or does she say 'kaput, husband kaput'? The policemen go away, and Bea and Jacob stand at the grave of the great, poor Mussorgsky, who drank himself to death, and can hardly suppress their laughter. Jacob takes his glasses off; his eyes are reddened from the cold and they are wreathed with laughter lines. He says, using ventriloquism, that it's so funny, one could die laughing, and the words seem to come from out of the grave. He almost shocks himself.

The two policemen are standing in the small guardhouse at the cemetery gates. As they go past, Bea

offers them Jacob's hip flask. 'Mediciiine, *spirtnoye*.'
The men take a large swig each. Laughter. Declarations of eternal friendship.

Outside the high wrought-iron gate crouch the poor babushkas again. They beg Jacob and Bea to give them a ruble or two, then they bless them and make the sign of the cross over them.

That evening in the hotel room Jacob massages Bea's feet and she rubs his tense neck because she has noticed how he keeps turning his head from side to side to ease it. His hip operation cannot have been completely successful: when he walks he drags his leg behind him and in the Hermitage he stopped quite often to sit down on a bench. Perhaps the scar hurts too. He wouldn't admit it, of course, but he too regrets having come to Russia in December. They order up tea and hot water bottles for their bed. In the freezing St Petersburg night Bea can kiss Jacob's scar, and he can lose himself in her hair as though he had no intention of ever getting free again. She lies safe within his arms and thanks God that they do not have a number tattooed on them.

On 29 December, at half-past eight (Russian time) in the morning, this time flying Aeroflot, they start their return journey. Going home. *Davay. Damoy.* Bea catches a glimpse of the cockpit as they board the plane. Two pilots, bearded and resolute, are standing in front of their impressive instrument panels. They look as if they play Russian roulette in their spare time. They greet each passenger with a slight bow, as if they were welcoming them to a cocktail party. Bea finds them about as reassuring as she does Jacob when he tells her that nowadays they have technical equipment to cope with all weather conditions. The snow doesn't affect this sort of jet at all.

While they taxi to the runway, the flight attendant hands out sweets and makes sure they all have their seat belts fastened. From her window seat Bea can see nothing but snow, *the snowflakes are three times as big as at home and three times as thick.*

When will she at last be able to tell Jacob her mother's story? Climbing through thick snow clouds, it is like breaking through pack ice. Along the outside edge of the wing the swirling snowflakes turn into hailstones. Bea sucks her sweet into a thin disc. St Petersburg has long ago sunk into the snow, or into the swamp out of which Peter the Great stamped it. Has Bea really been in St Petersburg? Or was it just a fairy tale, which will begin tomorrow with 'Once upon a time'?

This morning she woke up very early. Next to her, Jacob was still asleep, breathing quietly, not snoring, as though he were a child again, lying next to his mother, and had never been torn away from her and hidden in a hothouse and a wash-house. And now here he is, sitting the way well-travelled gentlemen sit, afraid neither of flying nor of being discovered. Now he is once again the unapproachable Doctor Stern.

The aeroplane drops into an air pocket, a snow pocket, it pulls out again and then drops again, and next to Bea Jacob seems not to have noticed at all, for he is making her a kind of proposal of marriage, that is, his hand is at the nape of her neck, he is running his fingers through her hair so that the hairpins with which she has fastened it in a low knot poke into her, and he is saying into her ear that this week spent with her in one room has been so astonishing that he could almost imagine being able to live with her, though mind you, he can't even live with himself. His hand draws back from her hair; the large horn pins both stay caught in the polo neck of her jumper.

'I'm sorry, I'm so clumsy. Will you be able to put it back the way it was?'

'I'll have to manage.'

145

Before Bea stands up, she takes Frau Hiller's notes out of her shoulder bag and asks Jacob to look through them, she found these pages a few years ago in a sealed envelope in the attic and since then –

No, she does not say 'since then'. She sways down the aisle without holding on to the backrests of the seats. She is floating on clouds. She knows that Jacob is looking at her. He could imagine living with her. Even if he did use the conditional, it sounded as though what he was also saying was what Bea's father wrote to her mother: *All my frailties can rest against you and my vulnerability is sheltered by you.* That is more or less what he means; of course he can think of nothing worse than always having someone around, and nothing worse than losing Bea again.

In the toilet, she puts her hair up. The mirror over the wash basin gleams in the neon light. Someone has scribbled on it in lipstick, complicated signs and symbols one sees nowadays sprayed everywhere on walls. Bea should not have just shoved the manuscript into Jacob's hand like that, she should have explained what it was in more detail. Is he reading the first pages, where Hildegard Hiller bravely set off with her sister, trusting completely in the Führer's empty promises? All the misery of being a refugee could not weaken her blind faith. Is he reading how the sisters had to look for a stable for their ill horse in a Pomeranian village? *The place was called Sageritz. It was a pretty village. Smoke rose from the chimneys. It looked very peaceful.* Does Jacob understand that the pitiful person who shared the attic room of the vicarage with

Frau Hiller and her sister was Bea's mother? Should Bea quickly go back to her seat and explain to Jacob that her mother was going to look for her father in the Stolp military hospital? But Frau Hiller writes that: *She had been looking for her wounded husband in Stolp. But the military hospitals had already been transferred west.* Of course, Jacob knows nothing about the telegram from Stolp, nothing about the young woman's panicky departure on 26 February 1945. Nothing in the world could have stopped her. She took no notice of her father, did not listen to the daily war reports on the radio any more, stopped reading the newspapers. She entrusted one-year-old Bea to her mother and left for Hinterpommern, just at the time when twelve million Germans were fleeing in the other direction. And Jacob does not know Bea's father's love letters, otherwise he would understand that her mother had no choice but to go to Stolp.

Perhaps he has turned over a few pages and is already at the next place, the name written in capitals and underlined, QUAKENBURG. *We arrived at a place called QUAKENBURG. Then four Russians were coming along the road, on bicycles. They surrounded us. Then we had to line up and be counted. Over and over again. Counting in Russian is* provertje. *Provertje,* a word which Bea says in her sleep. *An interpreter told us we would just have to be part of a labour force.*

Perhaps labour force was what they said to Jacob's mother too, when they came for her. Labour force, a phrase which falls far short of the truth. Jacob's mother. Bea's mother. The mothers crawl up sloping planks into the goods trucks. Frau Hiller makes detailed sketches, little lines of goods trucks, rolling along day after day, week after week. Eastwards. Always eastwards. Perhaps somewhere goods trains carrying liberated prisoners rolled past the women from the other direction. Perhaps the abducted women could see, through the small barred window in the other train, shadowy people who were on their way home, on journeys that history would call the death marches. Perhaps Bea's mother and Jacob's mother passed each other. Jacob's hope that his mother would return was like a clock and it was to go on ticking for a long time.

Is he skipping pages as he reads? Can he find his way through? Frau Hiller seldom noted down specific dates, and complains that her memory cannot keep track of the events in the order in which they happened. Only place names are fixed: RUMMELS-BURG, KONITZ. The farm. Woman come. *You can't write down how awful it was. And no one is interested, either . . . Ruth's green coat went as well . . . Ruth and I . . .* Then a sentence is deleted, struck through with a thick line, which Bea has tried to decipher in vain. Is Jacob holding the page up against the snowy light, trying to read at least one word? He would have to do that with a lot of the pages where the writing isn't easy to read, though on every page you can clearly see the watermark, the translucent picture of Bea's mother. *In Soldau Frau Bandilla said, 'God protect us, we're being abducted.' Ruth started laying into her. 'That's not true, that's not true.'* That moment, where her mother had to understand something that was impossible to understand, has so haunted Bea that it is she who beats her fists against Frau Bandilla's chest, and she who at some station or another in the middle of nowhere loses control and slaps a woman's face because she has changed the hands of her watch, which she managed to hide, to Russian time.

Someone is knocking at the door of the toilet. Bea has already stayed far too long in the bumpy little room. Perhaps Jacob is worried and has come after her, or the flight attendant wants to make sure everything is all right. Yes, yes, everything's fine. Bea glances again at the decorated mirror.

She goes back to her place; the aeroplane rises and falls in slow motion. Shortly after take off the passengers were asked to keep their seat belts fastened. Jacob has moved into Bea's window seat so he can see better. He has forgotten to fasten his seat belt again. He is in Korkino, or already in Kopeisk, a small camp, *no furniture . . . thirty degrees in the shade. In the night there were searchlights too.*

'You've forgotten to do up your seat belt.'

Jacob lifts his arm and lets Bea fasten his belt. He turns over a page of Frau Hiller's notes. Bea leans back in her seat and says she woke this morning at the crack of dawn and is going to try to sleep a bit.

She will be relieved when they have landed in Berlin. What they call turbulence up here is a snowstorm, which is shaking the plane about. If it carries on like this, Bea is going to feel as sick as she once felt on a roller coaster. But before it can happen she is blinded through her eyelids by the light above the clouds. They have left snow clouds, turbulence and wind beneath them and are gliding through the sunlight.

'You see,' says Jacob. 'I told you, bad weather doesn't affect a jet at all.'

Somewhere over Estonia or Latvia, Poland or what used to be Hinterpommern, Bea falls into a restless half sleep. In the soft hum of the engines she hears Auguste praying, '*Oly, 'oly, 'oly*, and she hears Frau Hiller mumbling her name. Have we been good and written something today? Green and yellow eyes stare vacantly into the emptiness. Bea wakes with a start and wonders whether she shouldn't take the pages from Jacob's hand before he reads the bit about the sick hut in Karabash. She would much rather have told him herself about what happened to her mother. Now he must imagine it for himself.

The sun sets in broad daylight. The plane plunges into fog and snow. Just before Bea's ears become blocked she hears Jacob putting the pages back into their plastic cover. She keeps her eyes closed. What will he say now?

Bea hardly dares breathe. The loudspeaker announces that they have descended from a height of ten thousand metres to two thousand and are preparing to land in Berlin. Soft music plays. Bea could now try out some ventriloquism to ask Jacob, without moving her lips, from a distance, to please find the right words. She breathes in deeply, holds her breath and tries to get the muscles of her larynx to vibrate. The plane bumps hard onto the clouds and shudders.

In a voice which sounds strangely choked, Jacob asks whether Bea has fastened her seat belt properly. She feels his hand at the back of her neck, supporting her head. He is waiting for her tears, so that he can dry them. That takes time, so the plane circles round and round above Berlin. It is never ending.

Jacob takes his hand from Bea's hair, carefully, so as

not to loosen the pins again. He reaches for her wrist, slips the watch off and sets it to middle European time. After that he does not let go of her hand.

The engines hum very quietly. They will start to roar again, but only when the wheels have touched the ground.